THERE IS A HOUSE

The publishers gratefully acknowledge the financial assistance
of the Arts Council/An Chomhairle Ealaíon

First published in 2003 by Marino Books
An imprint of Mercier Press
Douglas Village Cork
E-mail: books@mercierpress.ie
Website: www.mercierpress.ie

Trade enquiries to CMD Distribution
55A Spruce Avenue
Stillorgan Industrial Park
Blackrock County Dublin
Tel: (01) 294 2560; Fax: (01) 294 2564
E-mail: cmd@columba.ie

© Kieron Connolly 2003

ISBN 1 86023 152 7
10 9 8 7 6 5 4 3 2 1

A CIP record for this title is available
from the British Library

Cover design by Marino Design
Printed in Ireland by ColourBooks,
Baldoyle Industrial Estate, Dublin 13

THERE IS A HOUSE

KIERON CONNOLLY

for George and Eileen

Prologue

There is a house. It is old now, the memories of generations past long gone, memories which have escaped into the ethereal domain of winter's gloom. Once so grand and imposing, the structure is now a corpse, its skeletal remains having long since succumbed to the green swath of ivy which climbs its walls: foliage which serves as a reminder to all who might pass that the empty shell which stands before them is not of this time but of another; a mute witness bearing testament to that other time, the time when there was a living house in a place beyond the now, beyond reality. I know nothing about the house, save for the fact that it is part of my destiny. Its location is a complete mystery to me, but I know it exists. It has to exist. If it doesn't, I'm toast.

1

When I was in high-babies, Miss O'Mahony asked me a
question. It was a simple question – nothing too complicated.
Miss O'Mahony wouldn't ask me a complicated question,
because complicated questions are only for grown-ups, and I
was only five when the question was asked. Miss O'Mahony's
question concerned the future and my place therein. I gave
a great deal of thought to the question which was not
complicated, and using the three crayons available to me I
drew Miss O'Mahony a picture. I had a green crayon, a red
crayon and a yellow crayon, and my picture was full of green
and red and yellow. I drew a picture of a man in a space
rocket, and both the man and his space rocket were coloured
green and red and yellow. The sky above the man and his
space rocket was yellow, and it was home to a green sun
which had a scattering of red daffodils growing upon its
surface. Little people played in a garden which was adjacent
to the man and his space rocket, and all of the little people
had three or four eyes, but the man in the space rocket had
only two eyes, because the man in the space rocket was me.

The days passed, and the five-year-old became a grown-
up. He never got to fly in his space rocket: that's something
only five-year-olds do. No, he just became all grown up, and
started asking and answering questions which were much
too complicated. But he never forgot about the world of
green and red and yellow, a world in which anything is

possible, simply because it is. The five-year-old who was now a grown-up realised that he didn't need a space rocket to travel far away. Being the grown-up that he was, he knew that the world of green and red and yellow was slightly outside the norm. He considered going to a psychiatrist who was all grown up, but he passed on that. Little point in going to a psychiatrist, he thought to himself. A psychiatrist would not understand, he thought to himself. A psychiatrist would ask too many complicated questions about my space rocket, he thought to himself. Psychiatric help now rebuffed, the five-year-old who was now a grown-up did what he had to do: he jumped into his space rocket and became an author.

2

Today is not that different from any other day, beginning as it does with a consonant, and that consonant is 'T'.

Tuesday, interior, bar, lunchtime.

A clock sits upon the wall. The clock goes *tick-tock*. Occasionally it only goes *tick*, but that's OK. The bar is located adjacent to the River Liffey, no more than a stone's throw away from the Dublin street which is home to the General Post Office. Decades ago, in an Irish galaxy far enough away still to be ever-present, a small group of people gathered within the confines of that General Post Office. Too young to collect a pension, the one thing which they did have in common was a shared belief that yesterday would forever be superseded by tomorrow.

Yesterday came and went, as did tomorrow, and the present is nothing more than a stopping-off point for reflections on happenings which occurred once upon a time in the past, when the world had grown weary of youth.

Wars and revolutions come and go, and people live and people die.

History is written by those who have not been defeated, historians say.

Que sera, sera, Doris Day says.

The clock behind the bar goes *tick-tock*.

Today, the people of a proud nation walk by a General Post Office, some carrying credit cards, some carrying needles.

9

Independence proclaimed, we are now free to use both. Blood shed, aged youth long absent, we sit in proud judgement on our past, as we sit serenely in our present.

Once upon a time in the future, history will rightfully recall the small island which became an important part of the community of nations.

Once upon a time in the future, history will recall other happenings and occurrences: a needle here, a needle there. Youth forever absent.

History has yet to be written, some say.

Que sera, sera, Doris Day says.

Tick-tock, the clock says.

Idle reflections on things elsewhere.

I find myself reflecting on things elsewhere, because reflecting on things elsewhere is preferable to reflecting on things which are not elsewhere. History and Doris Day, the *tick-tock, tick-tock* of a clock.

Simple. Uncomplicated. I sit on a barstool, and looking into the mirror which is situated behind the bar, I see the reflected image of someone who is too terrified to face the nothingness which currently holds sway over everything else. The nothingness has a name, but it's best not to dwell on something so horrible. Writer's block is not an issue. I can write; it's just a question of finding something to write about.

Once upon a time, three months ago, the five-year-old who was now a grown-up signed a contract in which he promised his publisher that he would write a story which would comprise many words, and stuff that made some sort of sense. He also promised to have the manuscript completed within fifteen months. As is the way with these things, the days have come and gone, and fifteen months has now become twelve months.

The novel will begin with: 'There is a house.' The novel

will then build on its beginning, progress to its middle, and proceed to its end.

There is a house . . . The End.

Twelve months.

Shite.

(Memo to myself: Do not panic.) The important thing at times like this is not to panic. I have to leave the world of the present and take up residence elsewhere. I have to leave the world of two-eyed this and black-and-white that, and enter a multicoloured world of three-eyed this and four-eyed that. It is not such a strange world; it is the only place I know where all things are possible: a world in which anything is possible, simply because it is.

It is my world, the world of an author, and it is a world which is proving to be more than slightly elusive.

Twelve months.

Shite.

(Memo to myself: Panic.) The bar in which I sit is not pretty. The last time the front of this place saw a fresh lick of paint was probably the first time the front of this place saw a fresh lick of paint: a lick of paint which would have made its debut about ten years prior to the arrival of the American president who'd waved to the crowds as his motorcade travelled down O'Connell Street. Soon afterwards, the same American president would travel in another motorcade in another city in another part of the world. Shit happens.

Sometimes I reflect upon things a lot, sometimes not.

Sometimes I write a lot, sometimes not.

Sometimes I drink alcohol a lot, sometimes not.

I look into the mirror and I see a thirty-three-year-old author who mostly does sometimes a lot.

The clock is doing what it's supposed to do and goes *tick-*

tock. Occasionally, several times a day, it only goes *tick*. The singular *tick* will result in Jim the barman hitting the top of the clock with his fist; the clock then goes *tock*.

Jim is a barman who is currently in the process of cleaning a pint glass, and the cloth he is using to clean the pint glass will ensure that the pint glass will always be in need of cleaning. Jim the barman's lips are usually contorted, and resemble a flat basketball. This will lead to air escaping between the lower and upper lips of Jim the barman. Upon their release, the various molecules which combine to make up the constituent parts of life's breath will find themselves transformed into the gentle whisper which gives continual rebirth to a song called 'Danny Boy'. Jim the barman is sixty-seven years of age, and I have often wondered to myself if he might have happened upon something other than 'Danny Boy' in seasons past. In all probability, other songs and tunes would have passed his way, but none of them could ever challenge the predominance of the tune which has been the constant companion of the man who is currently cleaning a pint glass.

I look into the mirror and I see Joe the communist sitting on a barstool. Unemployed since he left school, Joe has not worked for forty or fifty years. Each day Joe has his pint or ten and somehow gets by. Joe believes that the Soviet Union was full of shite. His political beliefs are not dependent on the ebb and flow of history. All men are created equal – that's what Joe says. Joe usually doesn't say much, but when he says what he has to say it's usually worth saying. Joe's singular source of income is Joe's singular concession to capitalism: he is a tobacconist. Customs and Excise do not know about Joe the communist or Joe the tobacconist. Joe's place of business is wherever Joe happens to be, and the Marlboro Man would be proud of Joe and the aged coat he wears, a coat which also doubles up as a warehouse. Summer or winter, Joe always wears the same coat. Joe's coat gets lighter as the day goes by. A lot of people know about Joe and his coat. Business is business, Joe the tobacconist says. All men are created equal, Joe the communist says. I like Joe.

Jesus Christ sits in a corner of the bar. It's dark there and he feels safe. I can't see him in the mirror, but I know that he's there. He comes and goes, saving souls and sitting in dark corners. He dresses like you'd expect him to dress, except for the umbrella which he always carries with him. Doesn't say much, does Jesus: 'Thank you' is about the height of it, thanks he gives to Jim the barman for the bowl of soup he receives each day. Jesus wears socks with his sandals, and there isn't really much more that can be said about the Jesus who sits in darkened corners each day, partaking of his bowl of soup and saying, 'Thank you.' He is a mental-health statistic who fell between the cracks; a saviour who walks up and down Westmoreland Street each day smiling at passers-by. Nothing more for the saying, little more that can be said about the man who will share a smile with a communist of my acquaintance, following on from the daily receipt of a free pack of twenty cigarettes.

I look into the mirror and I see Frank the barber sitting on a barstool. Each day Frank the barber does what he has to do, which is drink. Joe usually doesn't say much, but Frank says even less, never discussing the demons from which he is constantly seeking escape. Frank the adult has always been a barber. Frank the child was in the care of the Irish state, brought up in an orphanage somewhere or other. No, never says much, does Frank. But sometimes I walk Frank home. It's usually late when I walk Frank home. Sometimes it's early, but it's usually late. Frank lives around the corner from the pub in which he drinks a lot, and it takes us no more than a minute or two to complete our journey.

Frank lives in a bedsit, and I sometimes put him to bed. More often than not, I'll wait for Frank to fall asleep before leaving. It's no big deal; doesn't take long. I'll sit on the single chair which is situated beside the single table in the single room which is home to my friend Frank, and I'll light up a smoke. TOBACCO SERIOUSLY DAMAGES HEALTH: that's what the Irish government tell me on my pack of twenty. I'D NEVER HAVE FUCKING GUESSED: that's what I tell the Irish government.

Frank has been known to fall asleep before his head hits the pillow, but I stay on for the extra minute or three regardless, smoking the smoke that will seriously damage my health. No, never says much, does Frank. But sometimes, as he lies on his bed with the scoreline reading: Frank the barber 0, Life 1, Frank will depart from those of us in the present and find himself magically transported to the past, to a time when words spoken were words ignored. Most of what he has to say is intended for a different audience, most of whom are now dead. They'll listen to whatever it is that Frank the barber has to say to, knowing that it isn't Frank the barber who's doing the talking. For the moment it is Frank the child who is tossing and turning on a single bed in a single room, and it'll be at least another decade or so before Frank becomes a barber. But as I continue to sit there, smoking the smoke that will probably kill me, listening to the nocturnal pleas of Frank the child, I realise that there are worse things than lung cancer.

3

In the past, there is a child.

He watched as Man United scored their eighth goal of the first half against Liverpool. It was an important goal because Man United 8, Liverpool 10 isn't as bad as Man United 7, Liverpool 10, and with half-time approaching, everything was now up for grabs. The match restarted with Liverpool immediately going on the offensive. One of their players jinked this way and that, that way and this, doing everything he could to elude the challenge of the two Man United players who had remained in defence. The Liverpool player passed the ball to another Liverpool player, who passed the ball to another Liverpool player, who picked the ball up and went home for his dinner. Match postponed due to circumstances beyond their control, the combined squads of Liverpool and Man United proceeded to run down the road, because that's what they always did. The child who was watching from a distance proceeded to walk down the same road, being ever-careful to keep his distance.

Grown-ups refer to it as low self-esteem. The child from the past simply carried on walking.

4

In the present, I remain seated at the bar, keeping company with Jim the barman, Joe the communist, Jesus Christ, Frank the barber and some guy called Tom. Tom usually has a lot to say for himself, but today he's saying little. He's just looking into the mirror, his gaze fixed on no one in particular. Truth be told, the no one in particular that Tom is looking at is the no one in particular who sits beside him, but I ignore both Tom and his gaze, hoping that they'll both do the decent thing and leave me in peace.

Behind the bar the clock goes *tick*.

Jim the barman stops cleaning the glass which is getting murkier by the minute and walks to the clock.

The clock then goes *tock*.

The *tick-tock, tick-tock* of the clock synchronises perfectly with 'Danny Boy'.

Nothing else can be heard: just the *tick-tock, tick-tock* of a clock, and 'Danny Boy'.

The articulated lorries trundling past outside do not break the silence.

Tick-tock, tick-tock.

'The pipes, the pipes are calling.' Nothing else.

'Gobshite.' No longer nothing else.

I ignore the remark, as does Jim the barman, Joe the communist, Jesus Christ and Frank the barber. Each and every one of us simply carries on doing whatever it was we were doing, which was nothing much, but sometimes nothing much is all you can do.

'God almighty.'

I say nothing; there's nothing to be said. There's a lot to be said for nothing.

'Have you *nothing* to say for yourself?' No.

'Paul, I cried. I actually . . . *cried*.' I'm sure there was something I could have said, but I didn't.

'What happened to you?' What happened to me? Good question. Fair question. No immediate reply forthcoming.

Tom O'Brien and Paul Conroy.

Friends.

Best friends.

Agent.

Author.

Tick. I suspect that it was the agent who was now addressing me.

Enter Jim the barman, stage-right.

Tock.

It was a television appearance.

A simple mistake.

Nothing more.

You see, once upon a time there was an author who lived in a land very far away.

Many strange creatures were to be found in this land, and they all lived happily alongside one another in a multicoloured landscape. But once upon the same once upon a time, the author was asked to leave his world of reality and move into the realm of something else.

But he did not want to move into the realm of something else; he wanted to stay with three-eyed this and four-eyed that, and colours which made sense simply because they did.

Nothing more.

The author was all grown up, and he knew about grown-up stuff and things, but now he was afraid because he was being told to go elsewhere. He did not want to go elsewhere because elsewhere was a television studio, and even though he was a grown-up, he was very nervous about things like that. So the author did what he had to do. Swallowing what little pride he had, or hadn't, he found himself confiding to a friend about the fear which had engulfed him. Now, this friend was a good friend, and a big friend: eighteen stone at least, and he did not come from the land which was very far away. He came from a land of two-eyed this and two-eyed that; a land where black was black and white was white. The author would occasionally visit his big friend in the land of matching colours and eyes which mostly came in twos, but he didn't stay long. Nice place to visit, he'd think to himself, but he wouldn't like to live there. The big friend listened to his little friend, but he didn't say much. He simply reminded his little friend that as he was now a grown-up, he should begin to act like other grown- ups. He also went on to tell his little friend that the time had come for him to behave like the brave little soldier that he was.

That's all that the big friend had to say to the little friend.
Tick-tock.

A television appearance.

Nothing more.

Once upon a time, no more than several hours ago, there was a brave little soldier who was big and strong and all grown up; he knew he was all these things because he had a big friend who told him that he was all these things. Truth be told, our brave little soldier was slightly nervous, because our brave little soldier did not like television studios.

Truth be told, our brave little soldier was scared shitless.

But something quite magical and wondrous happened to

our brave little soldier as he stood in the middle of that television studio, because he was to find himself looking up into the heavens, and as he did so, he saw something which went beyond all understanding. The lights above his head, which up until that moment had been nothing more than what they were – a collection of mundane electrical this and thats – were now something quite different. They had become messengers from the gods, and the instructions they brought with them could not be heard by mere mortals.

Their message began with *twinkle, twinkle little star* and it finished with *this is your moment to be a star*.

And message received, our brave little soldier became the *bravest* little soldier of them all.

Fear forever lost, replaced as it now was by a courage which surpassed anything that had gone before, the bravest of the brave was still looking into the lights which had saved him from fear, when he felt a hand tapping him on the soldier. Giving silent thanks to the gods who had forever altered his landscape, our gladiator returned to a world which had once been part of his reality. Upon his arrival, the first thing that Russell Crowe observed was the hand which had tapped him on the shoulder. It was a feminine hand, and it belonged to a lady who was carrying a clipboard.

'Are we ready to go then?' the lady with the clipboard asked the bravest of the brave.

Are we ready to go then? The man who would soon be a star knew that this could mean just one thing: it was now time to become a star.

So the man who would soon be a star did what he was expected to do.

In a distant corner of the studio, the bravest of the brave could see that a nice lady was talking to a nice man. In front of them were several television cameras, and as is the way with these things, the bravest of the brave came to the conclusion that the distant corner of the studio was where he should go.

Walking over this cable and that, and being ever-careful to keep the noise down to a minimum, the bravest of the brave then began to make his way onto the set. Behind him, the lady with the clipboard attempted to wish him well. In truth, her good-luck tap on his shoulder seemed overly aggressive, but she was most likely nervous too. At some point in the future, legend will have it that the bravest of the brave was not walking, supported as he was by the promises of gods who existed elsewhere, but it is of little importance. Whether he had walked or floated, the only thing that was of any consequence was the fame and fortune which would soon come to pass; promises which had been made once upon a time, when the stars had gone twinkle-twinkle.

And later – fifteen minutes later, to be precise – the man who would soon be a star was given his chance to shine. He was asked question after question after question about himself and his new book. But to each and every question, his response was the same: nothing. No one home; reality had left the building. The questions were asked, and the bravest of the brave simply smiled.

And far away, in another galaxy, an author's agent who went by the name of Tom O'Brien was crying like a baby.

Tick-tock.

Nothing more.

Shite.

5

In the past, there is a wallflower. No longer a child, he was now a traveller through time.

Map in hand, he had said goodbye to the child that he had been, and set forth on a journey to manhood. He travelled this way and that, that way and this, being ever-careful to keep his distance, knowing that he didn't belong.

In a city-centre nightclub, those who had once played football for Man United and Liverpool now found themselves dancing with members of the opposite sex. The music was young and alive, as were the teenagers who danced to it.

The wallflower who was no longer a child looked on, a soft drink in his hand. He too was young, and probably alive, but he didn't dance, because he couldn't dance. Instead, he did the only thing that a wallflower could do: he simply stood by the wall, looking on, a soft drink in his hand.

Once upon a time, that same night, there was a wallflower. Dancing temporarily suspended because of nature's call to the man who spun the records, the wallflower was joined at the wall by those who had once played football at the very highest level. The wallflower had never been on the first team, or the second team, or even the third team.

He simply was what he was, and sometimes that's all you can be.

'Jeezus, did ya see yer wan?' 'Fuck sake, lads. I'm tellin' yas, I'm in there!' 'Giz a tenner for da taxi.' 'Da knockers on her. Bleedin' hell!' . . . were some of the comments made by those who had just finished dancing.

There were other comments made that night, but the wallflower didn't pay much heed to them, preoccupied as he was by a question which had just been posed.

'Ya have, haven't ya? Go on, give us a swig' was the question posed, and 'Feck off' was the answer.

The discourse was taking place within a nightclub which was a meeting place for young adults who had left childhood and who were now ready to move on elsewhere.

Entrance was confined to those who had yet to reach their seventeenth year, and consequently, the bar didn't serve anything more lethal than soft drinks and crisps.

Question posed, question answered, the young adult who had replied in the negative now transformed himself into a conjuror who produced something quite magical from his box of tricks. Jackets were lying on the floor, their safety guaranteed by the presence of the wallflower who always stood nearby. Lifting up one jacket after another, the conjuror finally came across his own. Picking it up and reaching inside, he produced a bottle which contained something other than a drink which was soft. Unscrewing the top, he drank from the bottle. Guilt-ridden, he then handed the bottle to the friend he had snubbed and, swig taken, the bottle made its way from hand to hand, finally coming to rest in the hand of the wallflower.

Once upon a time there was a wallflower who didn't dance because he couldn't dance. Once upon the same once upon a time, the wallflower put down his soft drink and replaced it with something stronger.

Once upon the same once upon a time, there was no longer a wallflower; there was a man who found himself dancing and dancing and dancing, and everything worked out just grand.

6

In the present, the author's agent who went by the name of Tom O'Brien was looking at himself in the mirror. It was not an act of vanity. He was probably just wondering about stuff, and about how in hell he'd ever managed to get himself involved with the gobshite who was sitting beside him.

'I wasn't *that* bad, was I?' Some questions are asked, some questions are answered. Some questions are full of shite.

I wasn't that bad, was I? No, I wasn't bad per se. Not bad as in *evil* bad. I was bad in a psychotic, screwed-up, twinkle-twinkle-little-star kind of way, and people like me simply are what we are, and do what we do. Problem was, I did what I did on national television.

'Paul . . . ' My question which was full of shite was about to be answered. I knew this because I was looking in the mirror at Tom, and Tom was looking in the mirror at me. His face displayed no emotion; he wasn't happy, he wasn't sad. He simply was what he was: my agent, a fucked-up, quivering wreck who had once been a normal human being.

As I looked into his eyes, I could see what he was considering. From his point of view, the matter which was currently under consideration probably made perfect sense, and even if he was found guilty of murder, the judge would probably knock 10 per cent off his sentence on grounds of good taste.

'Thank you.' Jesus had moved out of the shadows and

was now standing beside me. Placing an empty soup bowl on the counter, he smiled at Jim the barman, and Jim the barman did what you'd expect him to do, and smiled back at Jesus. Jesus then headed out into the light, carrying the umbrella which he always brought with him. Closing the door after him as he went, Jesus stood outside the bar for a moment, and as I looked into the mirror which revealed all, I could see the outline of both Jesus and his umbrella silhouetted through the frosted-glass window which separated those inside the bar from the rest of humanity. Above the framed figure of Jesus and his umbrella was a sign that read: GUINNESS IS GOOD FOR YOU, only it didn't say that exactly; it said what it had to say in letters which were back to front, and which informed me that UOY ROF DOOG SI SSENNIUG, because that's what happens when you look in a mirror. Jesus then proceeded to head left, or right, depending on your point of view, bringing with him his umbrella, and a smile which would soon be making another appearance on Westmoreland Street.

Joe the communist and Frank the barber hadn't paid much heed to Jesus when he'd walked up to the counter carrying his empty soup bowl. They remained seated side by side, nursing the pints of porter which were good for them. Glasses half-empty, glasses half-full, they simply carried on as normal, doing what they were doing, which was nothing much, but sometimes nothing much is all you can do.

I was grateful to Jesus. He'd saved me, even if the stay of execution was only temporary.

Tom had opened up with 'Paul . . . ', then Jesus had made his appearance, and put a temporary stop to whatever it was that Tom had to say.

I wasn't that bad, was I? Tom had been asked the question. Tom had proceeded to answer the question and then stopped.

Tom clearly subscribed to the view that discussions between authors and agents should be stayed, pending the exit of Jesus stage-left, or stage-right, depending on your point of view.

'Paul . . . ' Tom clearly subscribed to the view that it was now time to continue answering the question which had been asked.

Shite.

' . . . how can I put this?' Fecked if I knew.

'Me agent, you author.' True. A blocked author, but true. There is a house . . . blah, blah . . . The End.

Shite.

'You write, I get 10 per cent. Simple.' Very simple.

'You starving, me starving.' Tom is eighteen stone. Tom is starving. Tom is talking through his arse.

'I did what I'm paid to do, and got you an interview on breakfast television. We're talking *prime-time* breakfast television.' Is there such a thing as prime-time breakfast television? 'A ten-minute interview which would give you the opportunity to sell both yourself *and* your new book.' Not untrue. Although the book wasn't exactly new. It was launched five months ago, and the sales weren't exactly good, bordering as they did on shite. In fact, it would be true to say that the copies weren't exactly flying off the shelves. More likely than not, if a copy was removed from a shelf, it was because someone had accidentally knocked said copy off said shelf, their foot being the most likely culprit. For reasons which were quite beyond me, the booksellers of this world invariably placed a book by Paul Conroy on the bottom shelf. Snow White may well have been intimately acquainted with seven dwarfs, but none of them shopped in Eason's, and the bottom shelf is not the place to be. The title of my latest novel is *Goodbye to Tomorrow*, and as of yesterday, it had sold eight hundred and forty-three copies. It would have been only eight hundred and forty-two copies, but a week after it came out I ventured into Eason's and bought myself a copy.

Goodbye to Tomorrow was to have been a story about this and that, that and this, but somewhere in the middle of the second draft, it changed its mind, and became more about this than that, and although I objected strongly to this sudden change in tack, the book ignored me, because that's what books usually do when they come into possession of a mind of their own.

'Paul, you were scheduled to appear at 7.35 AM.' True.

'I set my alarm clock for 7.20 AM. I woke up at 7.20 AM. Still tucked up in my nice warm bed, I turned on my television at 7.20 AM. Paul, I was *so* excited. Fifteen minutes, I can remember thinking to myself. Fifteen minutes, and my client, Paul Conroy, will be on television. Fifteen minutes. Not long. Just fifteen minutes. Anyway, I settled back and did the only thing I could do, which was wait. Fifteen minutes. Not long. Just fifteen minutes. Outside my bedroom window, the birds were singing *tweet-tweet*. That's nice, I can remember thinking to myself, birds *should* whistle *tweet-tweet* at 7.20 in the morning. So all is well with the world. The birds are whistling *tweet-tweet*, and looking at the television, I can see that a nice lady is talking to a nice doctor about strokes . . . ' 'Heart attacks.' 'What?' 'They were talking about heart attacks.' 'Paul, trust me on this one. They may have been discussing heart attacks, they may have been discussing strokes. Either way, it matters little. What *does* matter more than a little is that they were not discussing fuck-ups, and they should have been discussing fuck-ups, and do you know why they should have been discussing fuck-ups?' No.

I didn't actually say no, because to have said no would have involved the telling of a lie. I knew only too well why

Tom O'Brien had introduced a fuck-up into the conversation, but I kept my mouth closed; it was the only decent thing I could do.

'Paul, I'll tell you why they should have been discussing . . . ' 'You want another drink?' Clearly, the time had now come for me to open the mouth which was closed, and asking Tom if he'd like another drink seemed as good a way as any to do it. My reasoning was both subtle and cunning, and was performed with such sleight of hand that Tom would never notice. I wanted to change the bloody subject. I wanted to forget about what had occurred earlier that morning. I wanted to forget about heart attacks and strokes and fuck-ups. Best not to dwell on spilt milk. It was now time to dust myself down, learn from my mistake, and move the hell on.

'No, I do not want another bloody drink.' Sleight of hand or no sleight of hand, it was now quite apparent to me that Tom O'Brien was not ready to move the hell on, and that it would obviously be another decade or two before that spilt milk was put back in its bottle.

'So there I was, lying tucked up in bed, knowing that in fifteen minutes you'd be on television. My heart was filled with optimism as I imagined the conversations of the future. "Hi, I represent Paul Conroy," I would say. "Not *the* Paul Conroy?" "Yes, *the* Paul Conroy," I would inform Melvyn Bragg, and Melvyn would be impressed as he came to the realisation that I was the man who represented genius. Everything was well with the world. Fifteen minutes. Not long. Just fifteen fucking minutes. But then something strange happened. I noticed that the nice lady on the television had started to look confused. Why has the nice lady on television started to look confused? I can remember thinking to myself. And then I suddenly realised why the nice lady on television had started to look confused. The nice lady on television cannot believe what she is seeing. The nice doctor on television cannot believe what *he* is seeing. And what is this thing they are seeing? They are seeing a gobshite who has decided to go walkies on the set. Who *is* that gobshite? I asked myself. At first I can only see the arse of his trousers. Then the camera pulls back, and I can see that the gobshite is now standing in front of the nice lady and the nice doctor. "You're not due on for another fifteen minutes," the nice lady proceeds to inform the gobshite by means of a whisper, only it isn't a whisper, because the nice lady is incapable of whispering, freaked-out as she is at the sight of a gobshite who has decided to go walkies on her set. Fifteen minutes. It was 7.20 AM. I did the maths. In fifteen minutes it would be 7.35 AM. The birds had done the maths; maths which had put a stop to their *tweet-tweet*ing. Melvyn Bragg had done the maths. Melvyn Bragg had gone home. I was now staring at the television, transfixed. And then slowly, the gobshite turns and faces the camera. He is smiling; he is confused. I recognise the gobshite. My maths were not incorrect. I want to kill the gobshite. I want to kill myself. I don't know what I want, but whatever it is, it ain't pretty.'

Nothing more. Tom O'Brien had stopped talking. There was now silence, save for the *tick-tock, tick-tock* of a clock, and 'Danny Boy'.

Nothing more for the saying; little more that could be said. Tom O'Brien had spoken in length about the travails of Paul Conroy, and I then found myself doing the only thing that could be done. Ordering a pint for my friend and another coffee for myself, we sat together in silence, keeping company with Jim the barman, Joe the communist, and Frank the barber. Jim the barman would probably spend the afternoon cleaning a pint glass, whilst ensuring that time continues to do what time is meant to do, courtesy of a *tock* which is always preceded by a *tick*. And as he proceeded once again to tell the tale of a guy called Danny, all present would be grateful for the telling of the tale, for it rests easily with our reflections on things elsewhere; once-upon-a-time stories about a communist's belief in the equality of man, a barber's belief that the umbilical cord which binds his past with his forever will be forgotten about, if only for a time, and an author's belief that a television appearance with which he was associated had, all in all, gone pretty much as planned, save for the occasional panic attack.

The minutes passed, and as Tom finished off his pint, he had one final comment to make on the television interview which had, all in all, gone pretty much as planned.

'Shite.' And as I looked down into what was now an empty coffee cup, I found myself saying pretty much the same thing.

'Come on, I'll buy you lunch.' 'Thanks, Tom, but I'm grand. I think I'll stay here a bit longer.' 'Paul . . . ' Tom didn't say anything else. His best friend had just told him that all was well with the world, and that lunch could be stayed pending the arrival of a state of mind which would block out everything that had gone before. There were several reasons why Tom didn't say anything else, each and every one of them filed under pain and disappointment and worry: miscellaneous crap that could never be explained.

I looked at my departing friend, before turning my attention towards the mirror which revealed all, and reflected back at me I could see a world which had lost both shape and meaning: a landscape painted in black, and the place where I would often seek refuge.

7

If I had to guess, it was now Thursday, the day which followed Tuesday. My mind made a passing reference to Wednesday, but no such place existed, apart from the occasional glimpse or two – the briefest of perusals, which reveal nothing more than this and that – and conversations which may or may not have taken place. I awoke this morning at six o'clock. It was cold. It was a laneway. Consciousness returned, I stood up, only to fall down, only to stand up again, before eventually making my way onto Exchequer Street.

I hope the book is selling well, because I need a new jacket, a new pair of trousers and a new shoe. I'll probably need two new shoes, because I don't think you can buy just the one.

Six o'clock in the morning could just as easily have been six o'clock in the evening; the clock on Exchequer Street didn't elaborate. It simply did what it did, little hand pointing at six, big hand pointing elsewhere.

It was March, it was dark, and Exchequer Street was practically empty, save for the three down-and-outs who were sleeping in a doorway, in a street, at six o'clock in the morning. One shoe on, one shoe absent, I hobbled past them slowly, an absurd caricature who moved briefly within the realm of three down-and-outs: a brief period in time during which the three had become four. I moved on, not wishing to dwell on the situation which currently prevailed.

After making my way down George's Street, I turned left onto Dame Street. The occasional car passed by, but I looked away, because it was the only decent thing I could do. Most of the shops had their shutters down, and that was probably for the best, because I did not want to see a reflected image which would reveal nothing more than a man with one shoe on, one shoe absent, wearing clothing that had seen better days.

I was a writer and I was young and my life stretched out before me and I was fucked.

When the going gets tough, the tough do what they have to do, and I go away, seeking escape from life, if only for a while, a day or two at most. Theoretically, it should all make sense and work out for the best, but it never does. I leave and then return.

Sabbatical over, I survey my surroundings, only to find that the world got on just fine without me.

The man with one shoe on, one shoe absent exits Dame Street, turning right onto Parliament Street. An early-morning bus passes by. Behind the driver sits his only passenger: a middle-aged man who was probably making his way to a job which mostly entails the doing of something or other, in someplace or other: a daily routine grounded firmly in the mundane.

The man with one shoe on, one shoe absent is a writer who lives a life which is anything but mundane.

The man with one shoe on, one shoe absent would have given his one remaining shoe to swap places with the middle-aged man who had just passed him by.

The man with one shoe on, one shoe absent lives in an apartment which looks out onto the Liffey, and it is there that he is going. He had checked his pockets, and found nothing, which didn't really surprise him. It disappointed

31

him, but it wasn't a cause for surprise. Anyway, even if money was found, he'd have simply done what he always did, which was nothing much, which was much of the same. Sufficient funds would have allowed access to an early house in the markets, and he would have continued his escape from everything that had gone before, which was mostly Wednesday, although he couldn't swear to it. If he was lucky, his apartment might have some cash lying about, although it was unlikely, because that's what happens to a writer who spent the advance he received for a novel which would begin with the words: 'There is a house.' He finds himself crossing Capel Street bridge, Dublin's southside giving way to Dublin's northside. Stopping halfway between southside and northside, he hobbles over to the side of the bridge and looks down at the river beneath. One shoe on, one shoe absent, there isn't much more you can do at that hour of the morning. He looks down at the Liffey and he remembers. He remembers the time when he wasn't a writer. He remembers the time when life was less exciting, the time when he worked in a job of unrelenting boredom with a woman called Caroline Doran. He remembers falling in love with the woman called Caroline Doran, the woman who would become the mother of his child. He looks down at the Liffey and he remembers a lot of things: memories of the woman called Caroline, and the child called Jessica. Once upon a time he fell in love with Caroline and Caroline fell in love with him.

He remembers that.

It was thirteen years ago.

It was a Monday.

8

It was a Monday. It was one minute past midnight. It was Valentine's Day.

Joey the spoon looked at me. I looked at Joey the spoon. Elsewhere, a dog was barking in the distance. Joey the spoon was waiting for me to make my move. Elsewhere, a dog was still barking in the distance. Looking into the eyes of Joey the spoon, I could see that he was afraid – *very* afraid. I can't say that I blamed him. If I was sitting where Joey the spoon was sitting, *I'd* have been afraid. True, I was just a man like any other, but sitting opposite Joey the spoon, I knew that the sum of the parts which had combined to create the man who was now sitting opposite Joey the spoon included something more than simple flesh and blood. I was at one with the universe, and I was without mercy.

Death would soon be demanding that Joey the spoon paid his dues, and for him, there could be no escape. Nothing personal, Joey. Business is business.

Joey the spoon and me.

No contest. It was over before it had even started.

'So?' Joey the spoon had cracked. He wanted me to make my move, but Joey the spoon could wait a while longer. This was my moment, and the dagger which I was about to thrust into the soul of Joey the spoon was still in the process of being sharpened.

'So?' Joey the spoon was getting impatient.

'Jesus, Paul. Will you do *something*.' Tom O'Brien was now getting impatient, but Tom O'Brien and Joey the spoon could both go to hell. Death is not something that can be rushed into, and the instrument which would bring about the demise of Joey the spoon would reveal itself soon enough, because assassins dance to their own tune, keeping track of no one's time but their own.

'Fuck sake.' Paddy the Arab was now getting impatient. Tough. It would soon be time for me to make my move; soon, but not yet.

'So?' 'Paul?' 'Fuck sake.' Once again, the pressure was being applied by those who existed outside of my universe.

Joey the spoon wanted me to make my move. Tom O'Brien wanted to know if I still resided on planet Earth, and Paddy the Arab was making reference to seconds which had now become minutes.

Looking into the eyes of Joey the spoon, I knew that the time had now come. Only problem was, I didn't have a bloody clue what to do.

'I'll see your five and . . . ' I said to Joey the spoon.

Joey the spoon leaned forward in his chair, probably thanking God for small mercies.

Tom O'Brien leaned back in his chair, probably thanking God for something similar.

'Thanks be to fuck,' Paddy the Arab said, still referring to time forever lost.

'And . . . ' I continued.

'And?' Joey the spoon said.

'And?' Tom O'Brien said.

'Fuck sake,' Paddy the Arab said.

'And . . . ' I said, still looking down at the hand of cards I was holding: a pair of twos. Shite.

'And . . . ' I said, repeating myself, as I once again looked at the hand of cards I was holding: a pair of twos that were never going to be anything other than a pair of bloody twos. Shite.

Why the hell was I playing cards with a pair of twos? Why couldn't I tell Caroline that I loved her? She'd have probably been surprised to hear that I loved her, because I never told her that I loved her, and the reason why I never told Caroline that I loved her was because I was a coward. Simple really; nothing too complicated.

'And . . . ' I was still looking down at the hand of cards which would forever contain a pair of twos. Nothing more; just a pair of bloody twos. Shite.

At this point, all three of my playing partners said something. What they said exactly is unimportant; suffice to say that they all pretty much stayed in character.

'And . . . I . . . ' Matters were being advanced, much to the relief of Joey the spoon, Tom O'Brien and Paddy the Arab.

'I . . . fold.' 'You fold?' Tom O'Brien asked me, at just about the same time that Joey the spoon was clearing the pot from the centre of the table: money that was not destined for the Swiss bank account of an assassin whose card-playing abilities were on a par with those of a budgie.

'Yes, I *fold*.' 'You *fold*?' Tom O'Brien once again asked me.

'Fuck sake,' Paddy the Arab said.

'How can you . . . *fold*?' 'Tom, it was my hand, and I'll fold if I want to.' 'We were waiting *five minutes*, Paul. Five bloody minutes. In the name of God, you could have at least bluffed.' 'As I've already said, it was *my* hand, and I'll bluff if I want to, but I didn't bluff, because . . . another beer, anyone?' 'No thanks, Paul. Time I was heading,' Joey the spoon said, standing up from the table, en route to an appointment with a Securicor van.

'Is that the time?' Paddy the Arab said, still referring to time forever lost.

Once upon a time, a few years previously, Joey the spoon, Paddy the Arab and Tom O'Brien had all played football at the highest level. Sometime soon afterwards, I was to join them on the long march towards whatever comes next, thanks to a bottle which contained something other than a drink which was soft.

Joey the spoon was christened Joey Nolan. Several years ago, there was a sporting event which changed all that. Our school's annual egg-and-spoon race, a discipline which took courage, skill and other things which made absolutely no sense to me, had just seen the seven-year-old Joey Nolan cross the line in first place. It was the third year in succession that Joey Nolan had crossed the line in first place, and his success ensured that Muhammad Ali would forever be known as the second-greatest athlete of all time.

Joey was just minutes away from stepping onto the victory rostrum when the news broke: the spoon which had played such a pivotal part in creating the legend that would soon be Joey was a spoon that had just failed a dope test. The dope in question was glue, and the glue in question was the filling in the sandwich that was the egg and spoon.

Joey the spoon was shunned by everyone and anyone for several minutes, and Muhammad Ali breathed a sigh of relief. Joey was destined to carry that spoon with him as he progressed through life, a journey which would include a game of cards in which his opponent had nothing more than a pair of bloody twos. In time, Joey the spoon would become Joey the solicitor, and that's really all that can be said about Joey the spoon.

Paddy Lynch had red hair and freckles when he was a child, and that's how Paddy Lynch had found himself transformed into Paddy the Arab. Within months of the card game which occurred once upon a time in the past, Paddy the Arab emigrated to America and became a builder and joined the Republican Party and went mad. There's little more that can be said about Paddy the Arab. If he really did go insane, I wish him well when he takes up residence in the Oval Office.

Card game over, the four had become two, which was just as well, because the bedsit I called home was not large. There was a bed and a table and four chairs, the entire ensemble being topped off by a cooker, a sink and a wardrobe.

'So?' said he.

'So,' said I.

'Did you?' said he.

'Did I what?' said I.

'You know what,' said he.

'Do I?' said I.

'You do,' said he.

'I did,' said I.

'Fair play,' said he.

'Shite, Tom, I'm terrified.' 'Paul, how is the woman supposed to know about your feelings for her unless you tell her?' 'I can't tell her.' 'Paul, let us start at the beginning.' 'The beginning?' 'Yes, Paul, the beginning.' 'OK.' 'Two beers might be an excellent place to start.' 'OK.' 'And stop saying OK.' 'OK.' Standing up from the table, I walked to the fridge, which didn't take long. Three seconds later, I returned to the table, carrying two cans of beer.

Opening our respective cans, Tom began at the beginning.

'This girl that you work with . . . Caroline, yeah?' 'Yes, her name is Caroline.' 'And you love Caroline?' 'I do.' 'But you don't want Caroline to know that you love her, because you're a fucking lunatic?' 'More or less.' 'Paul, it's not as if you're some sort of social misfit.' 'I'm not?' 'You're not.' 'Honest?' 'No, I'm lying.' 'Fair enough.' 'Anyway, my point is, Paul, and I don't want you to take what I'm about to say too personally, but speaking as a friend, I feel it's something that must be said.' 'You do?' 'I do.' 'Well, whatever it is, I'm sure I can handle it.' 'Paul, you're mad.' 'I am?' 'Insane.' 'Fair enough.' 'Your behaviour around this woman is ever so slightly . . . nuts.' 'Nuts?' 'Yeah, nuts.' 'Well, nuts isn't too bad.' 'Paul, if you *do* love Caroline, it might be a good idea if you told Caroline that you loved her.' 'I can't.' 'You can't?' 'No.' 'Why?' 'Because.' 'Because what?' 'Because she might say no.' 'She might say no to what? A drink? A date? Dinner? Jesus, Paul, you don't have to propose to her.' 'I know.' 'You do?' 'I do.' 'And?' 'And what?' 'And what are you going to do about it?' 'I *did* do something about it.' 'Paul, you sent her a Valentine's card. In a few hours' time, she will receive that Valentine's card. Hell, I wouldn't be surprised to learn that she opened the Valentine's card. And do you know something? She might even read that Valentine's card.' 'You think? 'Of course I bloody well think. It's what people do.' 'I love her, Tom, but I'm scared . . . scared shitless. I see her, I need her, and I'm . . . I'm kinda fucked. Has anything I've just said made any sense?' 'Absolutely.' 'Which part exactly?' 'The part about you being a man, and her being a woman.' 'What part was that?' 'You're lost, aren't you?' 'I suppose.' 'You man, she woman. You in love, you screwed.' 'You think?' 'I do.' 'Shite.' 'Yep.' 'Anyway, Paul, there is no more advice I can give you. Things simply are what they are, and that's pretty much that.' 'Tom?' 'Yes, Paul?' 'What advice?' 'What do you mean?' 'You mentioned something about giving me advice.' 'I did?' 'You did.' 'I didn't tell you to join a monastery?' 'No.' 'Must have forgotten. It was Plan B.' 'Plan B? What was Plan A?' 'Plan A was simply more of the same. Accept the fact that you're in love with a woman who doesn't know that you're in love with her, and the reason why she doesn't know that you're in love with her is because you're

Paul Conroy, and in your world, things that don't make any sense generally don't make any sense because they could never make any bloody sense.' 'Shite.' 'Yep.' 'Are you going out with Caitríona tomorrow night?' 'Yes, Paul. It's Valentine's night, and I've booked a romantic, candlelit dinner for two. Rumour has it, that's the way these things are done.' 'Tom?' 'Yes, Paul?' 'Is my behaviour around Caroline that odd?' 'No.' 'No?' 'No, Paul, it's not odd. It's . . . let's see . . . no, odd doesn't quite do justice to behaviour that is reminiscent of *Fatal Attraction* minus the bunny rabbit.' 'That bad, huh?' 'Yes, Paul, it's that bad.' 'OK, thanks Tom.' 'You're most welcome.' '*Fatal Attraction*, huh?' 'Minus the bunny rabbit.' Tom finished his beer and headed off into the outside world. Tomorrow he would do what he usually did, which involved a visit to the Royal College of Surgeons, in pursuit of the medical degree which would make him a doctor. In time, a year or so on from the card game which had once contained a pair of bloody twos, he would become that doctor, and upon obtaining his degree, he would do what he was meant to do, which was to become a bookmaker. And in time, a year or two after becoming that bookmaker, he would find himself becoming an authors' agent, thanks to a bad day at Punchestown races, and the passing on of a manuscript which was his friend's first novel.

But the present does not allow the luxury of hindsight in matters concerning the future, and in the present, he could look forward to a day spent in the Royal College of Surgeons, followed by a romantic, candlelit dinner for two spent in the company of Caitríona, a girl who worked in a publishing house.

And that was that.

I loved Caroline and Caroline loved me.

Who'd have guessed?

9

And that was that.

The man with one shoe on, one shoe absent looked down into the Liffey. It had taken more than several minutes for the man with one shoe on, one shoe absent to remember the events of happenings past, and soon it would be dawn. He could not remember the future, because he believed that no such place existed. Instead, he made do with other things, content to block out the reality of his existence.

He loved Caroline and Caroline loved him.

He remembered that.

It was a Monday, and on that particular Monday Tom would have been doing what he always did, which was to look up his textbooks on all things medical, and I would have been doing what I always did, which was nothing much, but sometimes nothing much is all you can do.

Two years previously, I had left school, become a civil servant and met Caroline.

Simple, really; nothing too complicated.

Her name is Caroline, and she is beautiful. She is kind and gentle and considerate, and when she smiles at you, nothing else matters. The love story of Paul and Caroline is written in the past tense, but the beauty of everything that was and is Caroline is not confined to the past: it is something that will go on forever.

I had decided that I should tell Caroline about my love

for her, although I didn't tell her that it was me who loved her, because the Valentine's card which I'd posted to her was unsigned, and it seemed like a good idea at the time.

Good ideas at the time *are* probably good ideas at the time, but that time was long since past, and as I was now entering the building which was the workplace of myself and the woman I loved, I wanted to go home, which wasn't unreasonable, all things considered.

Entering the lift, I pressed a button. The doors slid closed, and the automated voice of an Englishwoman proceeded to inform me that I was now in the same ballpark as the first floor, and so on and so on. My tour guide finally stopped talking on the sixth floor and, stepping out of the lift, I bade farewell to the woman from England.

The room in which I worked was not small, and many people worked there. I'm not entirely sure who they were exactly, but I was pretty certain that some of them worked. I proceeded to walk towards my desk, saying good morning to most of the people who had managed to make it into work ahead of me, which was usually everyone.

Arriving at my desk, I did what I usually did, which was to sit down. I then collected my thoughts, only to give up the ghost on grounds of insanity. I had said good morning to almost everyone and anyone, although I hadn't said good morning to Caroline, because I hadn't looked at Caroline, because I was terrified.

'Morning, Paul.' 'Hello, Caroline.' The woman I loved had spoken to me, and I had spoken to her; she had also smiled at me. I know this, because I had briefly looked in the general direction of the woman I loved: a woman who was seated no more than ten or twelve feet away. She was beautiful, I loved her, and I found myself wanting to get reacquainted with the voice of an automated Englishwoman.

I looked at the clock. It was ten o'clock. The post usually got delivered to our desks at ten o'clock. There was no post. The post might have been hijacked by a group of people who hijack post because that's what they do. The post might not have been hijacked by a group of people who hijack post; it might have been making its way to Pluto, courtesy of an alien abduction involving aliens and an Irish Post Office van. Either way, I didn't care. There was no post, and I was glad that there was no post, because I was scared, and terrified, and ever so slightly screwed up. The absence of post was removing the terror which had been ever-present, and in its place there was something that I can only describe as terror.

Several seconds later, the absence of post was replaced by the presence of post. Frank, the man who delivered the post, entered the room, pushing a trolley in front of him. The trolley squeaked, and the letters which it carried were invariably bland, because that's just the way things were. That morning was slightly different, however. The trolley still did what it always did, which was squeak, but on the fourteenth of February, thirteen years ago, it also contained an envelope that stood out from the norm, and which was attracting quite a lot of attention.

The envelope was white, and larger than normal, and because it was Valentine's Day, my colleagues in the Revenue had done their maths, and correctly come to the conclusion that the morning post contained the usual assortment of tax returns, and a piece of post which probably made no reference to tax, returnable or otherwise.

Frank pushed his trolley, heading towards the desk of a woman called Caroline. One or two people had initially stood up and looked at the envelope which was not bland, and noting the name of the person to whom it was addressed, they proceeded to inform one or two or three other people

42

about the envelope which was not bland, so that by the time Frank had reached the desk of the woman I loved, he had an entourage, the likes of which hadn't been seen since the liberation of Paris, or Leitrim, or wherever.

Frank handed the large white envelope to Caroline. Caroline looked at the large white envelope and blushed. She also smiled, but mostly she blushed. Everyone and anyone, Frank included, was quite insistent that the envelope be opened. Can't say that I blamed them; I'd probably have behaved in much the same way, but I didn't have to behave in much the same way, because I knew what was in the envelope. It was Valentine's Day, and everyone and anyone, Frank included, would have known what the large white envelope contained too. But they couldn't have known about the verse that was written on the Valentine's card that was inside the large white envelope.

Only myself and the gobshite who'd written the verse would have been privy to such information, and as we were pretty much one and the same person, I wanted to go home, because I knew that my sad little verse was quite pathetic.

My love, my dearest love, it will have to suffice
That I say to you now, I will love you always.
Do not seek me out, for I am a coward.
A coward who will always, in his heart, be yours.

Pathetic. And yet there was nothing to be done, nothing that *could* be done. And so I stood up and joined my colleagues, resigning myself to a love that could never be. I could not have remained seated, because that would probably have meant giving the game away, and that was something I could never do. No, I just stood up and walked over to the desk of the woman I loved.

Caroline stood up, holding the card. She smiled; it was a smile to last a lifetime. For me, it would have to last a lifetime, as I was not about to give the game away.

Everyone was pleading with her to open the envelope; well, almost everyone.

Obeying their command, she opened the envelope, and slowly removed . . . my card.

Then, turning away from the assembled throng, she began to speak the words that had been written by a coward who simply was what he was.

As I began listening to her voice, I wanted to run away, but I knew that I couldn't run away, because even in the Civil Service, such behaviour doesn't go unnoticed. And so I just stood there, listening and dying, and feeling ever so slightly faint.

Slight hitch: I was listening to the voice of the woman I loved as she read aloud the words I had written for her. Problem was, the words which were currently being spoken weren't the words I had written.

'My love, my dearest love . . . ' that's what she *should* have said. That would have been grand. Shite, it was what I was expecting. I *wasn't* expecting to hear the woman I loved read aloud something which made absolutely no sense to me.

'I love you. I think that I have always loved you . . . ' were the words that Caroline read aloud, words which threw me into a state of total and utter confusion. I didn't know what was happening. I asked myself what was happening. I told myself that I didn't know what was bloody well happening. I thanked myself for being so helpful. Myself told me that I was welcome.

Caroline then closed the card and proceeded to inform everyone and anyone, myself and Frank included, that only two people would ever know its full contents.

I returned to my desk and sat down. I was shattered. I needed psychiatric help. I needed a drink, but I couldn't have a drink, because I only drank on social occasions, or at card games, or at weekends, or in nightclubs where you were expected to talk and dance. Shite.

Then, out of nowhere, or possibly somewhere, I found myself coming to an insane but logical conclusion. Someone had sent Caroline a Valentine's card which, verse aside, was identical to my own. But who? Putting one and one together, I came up with two, two being the person who was also in love with the woman I loved. Shite.

So Caroline was in love with someone, and someone was in love with Caroline, and that was that. I hoped that the someone in question would make Caroline happy, because the only thing that really mattered to me was her happiness. I also knew that my rationalisation of things as they stood was total bullshit, but it was the best that my mind could come up with.

Matter closed, albeit in a psychotic, la-la, run-of-the-mill kind of way, I sat back in my chair, knowing that there was nothing more I could do. This feeling lasted for about a second, before I realised that there was one more thing which needed to be done. I needed to ring in sick the following day, and the reason why I needed to ring in sick the following day was because it had just occurred to me that there were two Valentine's cards sent to the woman I loved. One of them had turned up, and one of them was still missing in action and was probably making its way to Leitrim or Pluto or somewhere. But knowing the Irish postal system as I did, I was only too well aware of the fact that the mistake would be rectified, and following a journey which would probably entail the taking-in of Donegal, Westmeath, Cork and

Kilkenny, the letter which had been posted the previous day, no more than three miles from my place of work, would arrive on Caroline's desk tomorrow, even if it was slightly jet-lagged. Valentine's Day had proven to be more than slightly screwed up the first time around, and I just couldn't find it in myself to be present when the verse which made a passing reference to unrequited love was put into the hands of the woman I still loved.

The day drew to a close with everyone saying goodnight to everyone else, but I was beyond faking it. I simply headed for the lift, and an appointment with the voice of an automated Englishwoman.

The lift arrived, the doors opened and I got in. In response to my pressing of a button, the doors were beginning to close; then they reopened, and the reason they reopened was because they were instructed to reopen, thanks to the pressing of a button outside the lift.

She stepped into the lift and smiled at me. I smiled at the woman I still loved, and we travelled together from the sixth floor to the ground floor, each step of our journey signposted by the Englishwoman with an automated voice.

No other words were spoken.

Outside, in the chill night air, I smiled at Caroline, and Caroline smiled at me.

No words were spoken. The silence between us was both simple and uncomplicated.

She went her way, I went mine. And that was that.

I walked home that evening, heading towards the bedsit which contained all my earthly belongings and a deck of cards which had once contained a pair of bloody twos. If she is happy, then I am happy – that's what I told myself more than once.

Truth be told, every couple I saw walking hand in hand

made me feel slightly pathetic, and very alone.

Entering the hallway of the house in which my bedsit was located, I closed the front door after me, and I was grateful to say goodbye to the world beyond, if only for a time.

There was a table in the hallway, above which was a mirror. I looked above the table and I saw a coward. I then looked below the mirror and saw some post lying on the table. Miscellaneous this and thats, the various letters were addressed to the people who also lived behind that front door. There was only one letter for me, and I picked it up, as you would. It was an unusual letter: white, and larger than normal. I opened the letter which was white, and larger than normal, and removed the correspondence which was contained therein. Strange, really, but I found myself looking at a Valentine's card. I opened the Valentine's card and read what there was to read, although I couldn't understand what it was that I was reading, because what I was reading made absolutely no sense to me:

> I love you.
> I think that I have always loved you.
> Perhaps you thought you were alone,
> But I can only say to you
> That your feelings of love run equal.

I read it once. I read it twice. I continued to read it. One and one suddenly made two.

I was two. There was no other two: just me. Caroline had not read my verse to her, although she had been holding the card I had sent her. She had read her own verse . . . to me. Only two people will ever know, she had said. I did the maths. Only two people will ever know. Caroline was one of those people and . . . I was going to do the maths again, but I couldn't, interrupted as I was by the sound of a doorbell ringing. I answered the door. There was no point in doing the maths again.

The answer was standing in the doorway.

And that was that.

And this was this.

Once upon a time, there was a man who owned two pairs of shoes. More often than not, he would find himself wearing his pair of black, leather-soled shoes, because his pair of suede shoes would only see the light of day when a summer sun came calling, and as this was something which didn't happen very often, he would usually stick with the pair of black, leather-soled shoes which had cost him £35.99, and £35.99 was a lot of money thirteen years ago. He also had a pair of Nike runners, although they didn't really count, because his white Nike runners simply were what they were, and did what they did, which wasn't much; but they looked good, and could be worn to the Olympics or Mulligan's pub, or almost anywhere.

Once upon the same once upon a time, there was a civil servant who lived in a bedsit in Ranelagh. Although his lodgings were small and cramped, they contained many things, including two pairs of shoes, a pair of white Nike runners, and a Valentine's card which had been the start of a love story which would last forever, give or take most of forever.

The thirteen years ago became ten years ago became the today which saw the man of the past transformed into the man of the present: a writer with one shoe on, one shoe absent, hobbling up the quays towards the apartment he now called home. Someone very wise once said that home is where the heart is, but broken hearts probably have no home, and his apartment was a lifeless shell, containing little more than a copy of the five novels he had written, a word processor which processed words that did not exist, and miscellaneous other items, although the one miscellaneous item that mattered most to the man who was hobbling up the quays with one shoe on, one shoe absent was a framed photograph of two people who were smiling. There was nothing or no one else in the picture, and that was as it should be, because a picture such as that is not usually the domain of a person with one shoe on, one shoe absent. One of the people in the photograph was called Caroline. He loved Caroline; he always would. The other person in the photograph was called Jessica. He loved Jessica; he always would, and besides, she was my daughter.

The man with one shoe on, one shoe absent continued on his way, and as he did so, he provided an early-morning distraction to traffic that would soon be rushed.

10

I stood outside my apartment block, waiting for someone to leave, so that I might gain access. My keys had gone the way of my money, and I had little choice but to wait. I suppose I should have felt some modicum of embarrassment, but I didn't. I simply waited with one shoe on, one shoe absent, feeling nothing, which was quite appropriate, because nothing or nowhere was the place I now found myself in. Vladimir to my right, Estragon to my left, we simply did what we did, which was to wait, hoping that he or she, or almost anyone, would open the door and let us in. Thirty or forty minutes later, the door opened, much to the disappointment of my two travelling companions. I'm not sure who they had been expecting would open that door, but I suspect that Kate Kowolski was not their first choice.

Kate Kowolski is a native of Thurles, County Tipperary. I once told Kate that she had an unusual name for someone who was from Thurles, County Tipperary, and she told me that Kate wasn't really that uncommon a name in Thurles, County Tipperary. I then went on to tell Kate that it wasn't Kate I had been referring to, and Kate went on to tell me that she knew I hadn't been referring to Kate, and I felt like a gobshite, but Kate simply smiled at me, before going on to explain that she had a grandmother called Teresa Ryan who went to work in England in 1938. Someone very wise once said that timing is everything, and in Teresa Ryan's case, timing was indeed everything, because a year after Teresa Ryan went to work in England, England declared war on Germany, and the rest, as they say, is history. Teresa Ryan's history included crossing paths with a young Polish pilot, who had made his way to England following Germany's invasion of his country.

The young Polish airman was to spend several years flying a fighter plane out of England and, countless missions completed, he would find himself returning to England alive, which is more than can be said for the majority, most of whom are now elsewhere, far away from the insanity of man.

Teresa Ryan fell in love with the young Polish airman, and the young Polish airman fell in love with Teresa Ryan. Because of the times they were living in, there was no guarantee of a tomorrow, and Teresa Ryan was to find herself becoming Teresa Kowolski sooner rather than later. The war ended, and the Polish ex-airman found himself looking east. Teresa Kowolski also found herself doing much the same thing, although east for her was west. Because love was involved, a compromise was called for, and so they headed west and raised a family in Thurles, County Tipperary.

Kate Kowolski lives on the same floor as me, and works for the Bank of Ireland, where she spends most of her day trading this currency for that currency, and that currency for this currency. She is in her early thirties and single, and drives to work each day in her Ford Fiesta, although that's really got nothing to do with anything. She also has superb taste in literature, purchasing as she did a copy of my first novel when she had worked in London about eight years previously. The novel was called *Dreams*, and Kate Kowolski was but one of a large number of people who bought a copy. Most of these people must now be dead, however, as all of my subsequent books have found it impossible to move beyond the bottom shelf.

Kate had informed me about her purchase within two days of my moving into the apartment block which was situated beside the banks of the Liffey.

'Hi,' she had said, as we passed each other in the corridor.

'Hello,' I had replied to the lady who was passing me by in the corridor.

'Excuse me,' she had gone on to say, as we continued to pass each other in the corridor.

'Yes?' I had replied to the lady who was still passing me by in the corridor.

'You're Paul Conroy, aren't you?' she had said, no longer passing me by in the corridor.

'Em . . . ' I had replied to the lady who was no longer passing me by in the corridor.

'I recognised you from the photo on the back of your book,' she had said, still no longer passing me by in the corridor.

'Em . . . ' I had replied, as one would.

'Please, just wait a second,' she had said, as she headed back towards her apartment.

I waited, and moments later she returned, proudly handing a copy of *Dreams* to the man who stood before her.

'Would you mind?' she had asked.

'No, it would be my pleasure,' I had replied.

And so it was that, two years previously, I had stood in a corridor with my new neighbour, signing a copy of a book she had once bought; a simple act which was to lead to the warmest of friendships. She would visit me, or I would visit her, and she would always make the coffee because I couldn't make a decent cup of coffee to save my life; or so she once said. She told me about her life, and I told her about mine. She told me about love found, love lost, love misplaced, and other things that made sense, and I told her about the two

52

people who smiled out at me each day from within the confines of a framed photograph; a reality which had come to pass thanks to a behaviour pattern that made no sense.

And now, two years on from the book signing which had taken place in a corridor, I was to find myself standing face to face with the woman who made a pretty decent cup of coffee. There was no one else present; the two tramps who had been my companions only moments earlier had decided to return to their world of fiction, waiting for someone other than Kate Kowolski to open the door.

11

Once upon a time, far removed from events which might occur in the future, I had sent a Valentine's card to Caroline Doran and Caroline Doran had sent a Valentine's card to me. What followed was a love affair involving a man and a woman, a relationship which evolved when time had stood still. Prior to Valentine's cards being exchanged, I had never known the difference between summer or winter, unaware of the fact that there was no difference; there was simply more of the same, every moment being a singular moment, existing within the confines of today.

Soon after leaving school, I'd jumped on a 16A bus in Beaumont and joined the Civil Service. Soon after leaving school, Caroline Doran had jumped on a train in Westport, and four hours later she was to find herself arriving in Dublin, en route to a job in the Civil Service.

She went her way and I went mine, both ways being the same way. For two years we sat together, working for the Revenue, and we were to find ourselves putting a date-stamp on post which required a date-stamp, and filing the files which needed filing.

Occasionally our paths would cross outside of the Revenue, as we sat with colleagues in the Long Hall or Mulligan's or wherever, as we celebrated the promotion of someone or other to something or other, or said a fond farewell to some mad eejit who would have made the decision to leave the Civil Service, opting for the world of fiction which lay beyond. But whether these social gatherings were consequent upon the receipt of a date-stamp which was larger than the one which had gone before, or a descent into a madness which went beyond all understanding, the result was always the same, involving as it did an inactivity on my part which belied the feelings I had for a woman called Caroline: a love which had grown stronger with each passing day. Cupid's arrow had taken off from Houston, and that was that. These events did not occur yesterday, or even the day before, and I cannot recall the exact moment when the arrow first struck, but I suspect that it was soon after my first meeting the woman called Caroline, and it was an impact which could probably be measured in seconds.

As is the way with these things, I was to spend a couple of years stamping and filing, dating and dancing, a soft drink long since absent. The wallflower within had, for the most part, largely disappeared, and in his absence I was now a man who was young, free and single. But when it came to Caroline, the wallflower within would invariably return, insisting that I keep silent, as he reminded me of a truth concerning myself: a simple reality which made a passing reference to a self-confidence which was notable by its absence, except for those moments when I came into contact with something other than a soft drink.

Caroline once told me that she knew I was shy, but that was OK. She also once told me that she loved me simply because she did, and I guess that's OK too. In time, Houston would confirm that Cupid had lifted off, thanks to a Valentine's Day which had come to pass, once upon a time when I was young. In time, a message would be forwarded to Houston, alerting them to a problem that had developed; but this is the past, and as such, the problems of the future had yet to occur.

12

Once upon a time I was not born. In a distant place, far removed from things which are complicated, I was at peace. Perhaps, at some time in the future, or so I once thought, I would return to an existence which exists beyond today, the warmth of a mother's womb having been replaced by the warmth of a nothingness which defies all understanding.

Perhaps, at some point in the future, as I now know, things aren't quite as complicated as they once seemed.

I awoke from a sleep that had never occurred, because sleep does not come easily when you find yourself in the middle of a game reserve, marking time with an assortment of animals, most of whom are small and fleet of foot. It was difficult to say where they came from exactly; they seemed to favour the four walls which were surrounding me, but that's probably because I was mad. To be a man, someone once said, you simply had to lose everything on the toss of a coin, and do whatever comes next.

But it's difficult to be a man when you're lying in bed, wearing a pair of pyjamas and a safari hat, watching the animals go by.

Earlier that day, or the day before, Kate Kowolski had opened the door and let me in.

What followed was a conversation between two people – a discourse without words. She had taken her neighbour by the arm: a gesture which was not accompanied by condemnation. She simply did what she did, which was something she didn't have to do, and accompanying a man with one shoe on, one shoe absent, we had set forth on a journey which would see me returning to the place I called home, thanks to the spare set of keys I had once given to a neighbour called Kate Kowolski.

In my kitchen there was a table, and it was there that I sat. Elsewhere, in a world beyond fact, two tramps had returned to a tree, waiting for someone other than Kate Kowolski to show up. I envied those tramps, because they knew what they wanted, which was to wait, and sometimes waiting is all you can do. I also wanted to wait, hoping that sometime soon, dignity might make its return, but to have waited would have been pointless, for dignity is something only given to tramps who wait and other members of the human race, not to people with one shoe on, one shoe absent.

As I sat at the kitchen table with the neighbour who had once bought one of my books, I knew that it would soon be time for the animals to make their appearance; they always did. But for the moment they would also wait, content to bide their time, withdrawing into the shadows, in anticipation of the withdrawals to come.

I sat at the table with my neighbour. Kate Kowolski had made me a cup of coffee.

I lifted the cup. The coffee inside the cup shook. My neighbour then stood up from the table and lifted the cup. The coffee no longer shook. I drank the coffee.

Kate Kowolski has black hair, is five foot six inches in her bare feet, and is my wife. I love her and she loves me, but none of that has yet happened, because this is only Chapter 12, and I suppose that I'm not really supposed to refer to things like that in Chapter 12. The one thing I will say is that I wrote Kate Kowolski a letter. It is but a single letter in a long line of letters, and I think I wrote it yesterday, several years on from the coffee that didn't shake. The letter simply was what it was, which was a letter, and sometimes that's more than OK, because I love the woman who was once my neighbour, and that's why I wrote the letter.

I love you, Kate. I love you for being you. I love you for saying yes. I was terrified when I asked you that question. You could have said no, but you didn't. You said yes, and I'd just like to thank you for saying yes. I love waking up in the night, knowing that you are beside me. I love you for caring so much about the people from the past, people who are also very much part of my present. I love the way I can't make a cup of coffee to save my life, and you can. I love the way you can dance, and I can't. I love seeing your smile in the morning. I love seeing your smile at night. I love seeing your smile most anytime. I love knowing that there was a time when I didn't know you, because it serves as a reference point for everything that has happened since, and everything since has been wonderful. I love you for many reasons, but most of all I just love you for being you: the woman who once said yes.

A letter which is written in the sands of time must forever be erased, if only for today, because those who know about these things say to those who do not that everything is defined by the certainty of what once was, ignoring the possibility that everything that might come to pass may already have done so, past, present and future being one and the same. We are Alice, and we see what we see, sometimes forgetting that the looking-glass through which we gaze is slightly distorted, ignoring as it does the memories which drift in from some distant place in the future.

In an alternative universe, an editor might possibly be forgiven for querying the arrival of a love letter which belongs to another time, another place, but fact is fact, and fiction is fiction, and always the twain shall meet.

Sometime prior to the writing of a love letter that refers to a time in the future when things might possibly change, I stood up from my kitchen table, only to sit down again. I had little choice, for to remain standing would have involved collapsing, and consequently, sitting seemed like a pretty reasonable thing to do.

I sat in silence with my neighbour for several more minutes. No words were exchanged, because no words could be exchanged. I simply did what I did, which was to finish drinking a cup of coffee. And Kate Kowolski simply did what she did, which was to hold the cup that contained the coffee.

In time, I would stand up from the table, assisted by the woman who was my neighbour.

Side by side, we would then walk slowly towards the bedroom. Truth be told, Mills & Boon had no part to play in the scene which was unfolding, sidelined as they were by the animals which would soon come calling. Upon entering the bedroom, my neighbour put me sitting on the side of the bed, as hands which should have been pressing the buttons which traded this currency for that currency, and that currency for this currency, now found themselves performing a quite different task, removing, as they did, the battle-scarred jacket off the back of a man who was her neighbour.

She then left for a moment or two, before returning with a pair of pyjamas which were coloured green and red and purple and orange. With the benefit of hindsight, I now know that Kate Kowolski usually sleeps in oversized pyjamas, the colours of which are mostly mad, but hindsight was not available to me, once upon a time, when the animals would soon come calling.

Putting the mad pyjamas on the bed, Kate Kowolski

returned to the kitchen, and I was to spend more than a couple of minutes removing clothing which had seen better days, before crawling into bed, wearing a pair of pyjamas which were coloured green and red and purple and orange.

I then proceeded to sleep the sleep which had never occurred, wearing the pair of mad pyjamas which belonged to my neighbour Kate Kowolski.

13

Outside, darkness had fallen, and the stew contained potatoes and meat and several vegetables. Kate Kowolski had not gone to work that day, the world of finance giving way to a world of neighbourly kindness. The animals had come and gone, and I now found myself reflecting on the happenings of the recent past, unable to remember a thing.

A grown-up, I sat at my kitchen table, wearing a dressing gown and a pair of mad pyjamas. In my right hand there was a spoon, and on that spoon there was some stew.

The spoon had a simple task to perform; nothing too complicated. It simply did what it did, which was all it could do, but the task it had been assigned – namely the transportation of stew from plate to mouth – was not made any easier by the turbulence which had occurred, once upon the time, when every nerve in my body had shaken.

'How are you feeling?' she asked me, a query which had been accompanied by a smile. I cannot recall if I replied to Kate Kowolski. I'm not sure what I could have said. I probably just sat there in silence, slowly eating the stew which had been made by the woman who might someday be my wife.

14

Kate Kowolski went to work on Friday morning. She looked in on me before she left.

She asked me how I was doing, and I told her that I was doing fine, which was mostly a lie. I felt like a bucket of shit, but there you have it. She then asked me how I was really doing, and I told her I was doing fine, which was still mostly a lie. She smiled at me before she left, heading off for the Ford Fiesta which was parked in the garage beneath, and which had an L-plate on the front window and an L-plate on the back window. She once told me that she had failed her driving test three times. I asked her why she had failed her driving test three times, and she told me that it was because she hadn't sat her driving test four times, which seemed like a pretty reasonable answer at the time.

At some point in the future, Kate Kowolski will pass her driving test on her sixth attempt, but that hasn't happened yet, and so it doesn't really matter.

Paul Conroy also went to work on Friday morning. I looked in on myself before I left.

I asked myself how I was doing, and I told myself that I was doing fine, which was mostly a lie. I felt like a bucket of shit, but there you have it. I then asked myself how I was really doing, and I told myself that I was doing fine, which was still mostly a lie.

In my bathroom there is a mirror, and in that mirror there

was a face. The face had many colours, mostly black and blue. I didn't really need to ask myself how I was doing, because some things are self-evident, and the face which had looked back at me was more than sufficient evidence of self.

Questions asked, questions answered, I headed off to work, arriving several seconds later at a word processor which sat in the corner. Beside the word processor there was a phone, and on the phone there were some messages. Sitting down in front of the word processor, I ignored both the phone and the messages which would inevitably have been waiting for me, and besides, I didn't have to lift the phone to know that there were some messages waiting for me. I had taken a walk on the wild side, a stroll down memory lane which usually excluded memory, and my excursions would inevitably see me meeting up with animals which were mad: a sequence of events which would result in people trying to contact me, if for no other reason than that they cared.

My mind and body were still reacting to events which had occurred elsewhere, but it was now time to get down to work, and soon after flicking on the switch which brought life to a word processor that defied the trade descriptions act, I was to find myself looking at a screen. On that screen there were some words: a sequence of letters which were mostly composed of shite. I was familiar with these words, but I could not understand them, and I doubted very much if they could understand me.

There is a house, I was told.

I was also told some other things, all of which could be filed under the aforementioned shite.

The house is old, and there is nothing more that can really be said about that house.

The cursor on the screen went *blink-blink*. I told it to go away, but it wouldn't. It simply carried on doing what it was doing, each *blink* of its *blink-blink* mocking me, as I sat, impotent, waiting for the arrival of words which would never exist.

And so I sat there doing nothing, and sometimes nothing was the best I could do.

The silence was broken by the sound of my phone ringing, and I decided to answer the phone, because I figured that the answering of a phone was preferable to what I was currently doing, and what I was currently doing was nothing, and even nothing was something of an exaggeration.

Tom told me about the messages he'd left, and I told him a lie. I told him that I hadn't received any messages, probably because my phone was broken. He then queried me on the answering of a phone that was broken, and I told him I wasn't a rocket scientist.

Sometime soon afterwards, the phone rang again. It was Caroline. She made a passing reference to the messages she'd left, and I told her I was screwed.

15

I sit in St Stephen's Green, looking at a duck. It is lunchtime, and the duck is eating some bread. Elsewhere, in another part of their universe, another duck sees the duck eating the bread, and decides it's lunchtime. And so the hungry duck glides over towards the duck who is dining, and on the face of it, everything seems to be OK. Below water that is not blue, the hungry duck's feet are probably going like the clappers, but what you see is what you get, and what you get with the hungry duck is a demeanour which gives nothing away. He is simply a duck like any other duck, and because of this he wants some food. The dining duck is probably a western duck, because he doesn't want to share the food, something he makes clear with the aggressive flapping of wings, and a squawk which suggests that he smokes too much.

In time, the hungry duck will probably regroup, and attack the dining duck who wouldn't share the food, and the dining duck will express genuine surprise at the violent actions of the hungry duck, and I guess that's probably the way of things in a pool that is putrid.

I sit on a bench, looking at things elsewhere. Beside me sits Tom. He owns 10 per cent of me, and I'm guessing that he now wishes it was 9 per cent. In the telephone conversation that referred to messages left, and a career that did not include the science of rockets, Tom had suggested that we meet for lunch. I said fine, maybe in a week or two. I told him that I was writing, and that I wanted to go with the flow. Tom told me I was talking shite, and so I met him for lunch.

And so we sit on a bench, sharing a sandwich. In front of us the world goes by, people coming and going, ducks squawking, not talking. I had been the first to arrive.

Several minutes later, I was to see Tom approaching. The nearer he got to me, the less he wanted to see. The thirty feet between us became twenty feet, became two feet, until he stood in front of me and said 'Christ.' He then sat down beside me and said 'Fuck.' Myself and my agent hadn't really got that much to say to each other. He handed me half of his sandwich, and I cried. Little boy blue had lost his shoe, and sanity wasn't far behind. Tom then made the briefest of references to a friend who was lost, and made some absurd comment about alcoholism. He then gave me a hug.

Little boy blue had indeed lost his shoe, beaten to a pulp by a wallflower.

16

Sometime soon after joining the Civil Service, I said goodbye to the home of my childhood, embracing the world beyond. My new world was a small room in Ranelagh, which the landlord described as a bedsit. I shared the house with Shane and Sheila and Frank and Deirdre. Shane and Deirdre were students who did feck all, and the rest of us were civil servants who did something similar.

Within weeks of moving into my new abode, I had developed a full-blown crush on Sheila, which in truth was only half-blown, because Sheila got a transfer and went home to Ballina – a move that was totally unrelated to the afore-mentioned crush, whatever its size.

I didn't know that Sheila had gone home to Ballina until I knocked on her door one night, but if I had known, I'm not sure what I would have done, but I didn't, so I did.

Knock-knock, said the door. I stood outside the door, waiting for Sheila to answer.

It was Wednesday night, and there was nothing on television except for Brian Farrell, which pretty much goes to prove my point. Plucking up what little courage I had, or hadn't got – I couldn't really be sure, and it didn't really matter – I decided to ask Sheila if she fancied going out for a drink with me, figuring that she'd probably prefer to spend an hour in my company than spend it in the company of a man who was much too old for her.

Knock-knock, said the door, following on from the *knock-knock* that had preceded it. Eventually, Sheila managed to drag herself away from Brain Farrell and, answering the *knock-knocks* that had gone before, she opened the door. Sheila was attractive, had fair hair, and was about three inches shorter than me. She also had clean fingernails.

However, the Sheila that now stood before me was anything but attractive, had black hair, and was about six inches taller than me. She also had fingernails that were mostly not clean, because they were now mostly black. Also – and this point is not unimportant – Sheila was now a bricklayer called Tommy, and it turned out that the bricklayer called Tommy had moved in earlier that day, taking the place of the woman who had gone home to Ballina.

In the absence of Sheila, I was forced to make do with Tommy, and the two of us went for a pint, and I turned up late for work the next day because I was young and free and single.

Two years on from the absence of Sheila, I was still mostly young, and although technically still free and single, I was neither, because Caroline loved me and I loved Caroline. My bedsit in Ranelagh, a residence that had previously contained two pairs of shoes and a pair of Nike runners, was now home to about ten other pairs of shoes, none of which fit me, and even if they did, the high heels that some of them possessed would have made walking extremely difficult, and my wardrobe was also severely compromised, overrun as it was by dresses and skirts and jumpers that were mostly woolly.

But none of this mattered, because Caroline loved me and I loved Caroline, and for the first time in my life, I was a man who had found happiness amongst shoes that were many, and jumpers that were mostly woolly, and I guess that's a small price to pay for love.

17

Jessica, my daughter, will soon be twelve years of age. She is now a young woman, and her mother tells me that my daughter's hormones have gone mad, which is pretty much the way things are meant to be, I suppose. I haven't seen my daughter for two years, much to the disappointment of the woman who gave birth to her. The exile is self-imposed, and is based entirely on logic. The way the story goes, Jessica has a father who is on occasion something of a fuck-up: a man who could never predict the day or the hour when he would decide to say goodbye to the world, if only for a time. But I came to the conclusion that a child should never be exposed to behaviour that is insane at best, and irresponsible at worst, and because I love my daughter, I decided to leave, knowing that it was the only thing that could be done.

When my daughter was a child, which she still is, I used to sit beside her cot and read fairy stories to her. She slept with a plastic tomato called Domato, and Domato used to play a jingle, thanks to the pressing of a button that was on top of Domato's head. I think the jingle was the signature tune from *The Magic Roundabout*, but I couldn't be certain.

It might have been a jingle from something other than *The Magic Roundabout*, but the more I think about it, the more certain I become that it was probably the jingle from *The Magic Roundabout*, although I could be wrong.

Regardless, she was an infant, and Domato was a tomato,

and I'd sit beside their cot and read fairy stories to them. All of the stories had happy endings, much to the delight of Domato. My infant daughter was mostly unaware of the endings that were happy, having fallen asleep somewhere around page three or four. Story told, beauty now sleeping, I would lean into the cot and kiss my daughter goodnight. Sometimes – in fact, usually – I would wait a minute or two before turning off the light, spending what seemed like an eternity looking down upon the child who would now be sleeping with a tomato called Domato.

18

Caroline sits across the kitchen table from me. Several hours on from my lunch with Tom, I sport a face that is still bruised, and an empty spirit.

Prior to my lunch with Tom, I had given up on the novel which would begin with the words 'There is a house', and with little else to do, I picked up the phone and listened to the numerous messages which had been left for me.

Some of them were from Tom, and the remainder, bar one, were from Caroline.

The bar-one message had been left by a man who worked for a bank, and who wanted to know about the overdraft he had not sanctioned. I thought it might be best if I returned his call, and pencilled in Wednesday three weeks as the most appropriate time to do so.

The first message that Tom had left was simple enough: a query which enquired into my current state of health, and all of his subsequent messages said pretty much the same thing. Caroline's messages followed a similar pattern to those of Tom's, although Tom made no reference to going out of his head with worry.

Caroline had heard of my latest walk on the wild side thanks to a bush-telegraph which had made reference to same: a telephone call which had been made by my agent and best friend to the woman who was the mother of my child, and who once owned many pairs of shoes, and jumpers that were mostly woolly.

Having listened to the messages that had been left, I hung up the phone and proceeded to do the only thing I could do, which was nothing much, but sometimes nothing much was all I could do. I simply sat on the chair which was situated in front of a word processor whose screen was now black, and lit up a smoke, and therein lies the true horror.

It is not the bruises that hurt, because in time, a week or two at most, the bruises will disappear, and facially everything will return to normal; normal being a cross between Liam Neeson and Woody Allen.

It is not the sleep that never occurs that hurts, because in time, a day or two at most, the animals will have retreated, and sleep will slowly return, if for no other reason than exhaustion.

No, the horror lies elsewhere, and it can best be found in the silence of an empty room, where one finds time to reflect, and where nothing much happens, because you are now nothing.

Que sera sera, Doris. Tell me about it.

Caroline now sits opposite me and asks me how I am. Earlier that day, I had sat in St Stephens Green with a big man called Tom, and I had cried. I now find myself sitting opposite the woman I will always love, and tears do not flow, which is a bit arse-about-face, but there you have it. I simply sit opposite Caroline and tell her that I'm basically screwed, which isn't a lie, or a request for sympathy. It simply is what it is, and the man who sits opposite Caroline is doing nothing more than stating the obvious.

Caroline is no longer a civil servant. A couple of years after Jessica was born, she joined the ranks of the mad eejits who had gone before, forsaking the world of filing this and date-stamping that for whatever might lie beyond. Opening a little shop that sold sandwiches to people who worked in the city centre, she was to find herself selling quite a lot of sandwiches to quite a lot of people, and a couple of years after opening the little shop, she closed it and opened a big shop, and the big shop became two big shops, which became two coffee shops, which became two restaurants.

A year or so after Caroline went mad, I too joined the lunatic asylum and jumped ship, thanks to the publication of a novel called *Dreams*, a story about this and that, and that and this, each and every one of its eighty thousand words written in the flat which I shared with a woman called Caroline, an infant called Jessica, and a tomato called Domato.

Caroline asked me how I was feeling.

I did not reply, because there could be no reply.

Caroline then did the only thing she could do, which I guess was OK. Standing up, she walked around to my side of the table and gave me a hug, and I made a sacred promise to myself that the animals would never come calling again.

19

Today is my daughter's twelfth birthday. It is several weeks since the animals bade me a fond farewell, and my life now begins on Monday and ends on Sunday: days which are seven in number, and which are best remembered simply for being remembered. I am no longer mad, thanks to the drinking of coffee and an occasional soft drink.

I sit at the bar. The clock goes *tick-tock*, and everything is as it should be. Minutes earlier, Jesus had said 'Thank you' and gone on his way.

I sit at the bar, keeping company with Joe the communist, Frank the barber and Jim the barman. Sanity has enabled me to start writing again, and back in my apartment there is a work in progress which begins with the words 'There is a house.' The novel is small, and it has yet to reach page two, but I'm not that concerned, because page two will come in its own time, and page three can wait, pending the arrival of the page that went before.

On the bar counter, there sit two pints of stout and one soft drink. I ignore the two pints of stout, not wishing to dwell on them, preferring instead to focus my attentions on a drink that is black and fizzy and soft.

Beside my drink there is a present. It is for my daughter, because she is now twelve.

In recent weeks, I have spoken to her mother each day, and each day her mother has invited me to the birthday party that is being held in the house I used to call home.

Tonight the house will be full of girls who are friends of my daughter, and there will be much happiness as they celebrate a birth which occurred at four in the morning, twelve years ago, on the fourth floor of the Coombe Hospital.

Seven hours prior to the birth, I had been sitting beside an expectant mother, watching the news on television. I'm not sure if the news had been good, bad or something in between, and I didn't really care, because I knew that in about a week's time I would become a father, and that was really the only news which was of any concern to me.

Then out of nowhere, or possibly somewhere, there was a newsflash, which took the form of news which had decided to break one week ahead of schedule, and I remained calm, and acted like any man would in similar circumstances, which more or less speaks for itself.

One panic attack, one taxi ride, and another panic attack later, I walked into the Coombe Hospital with Caroline, and she told me that I'd be grand, which I was. The nurses were very nice, and they gave me a cup of tea and two biscuits, and they also told me that I'd be grand, which I was.

I was present when my daughter was born, and she was covered in mush and stuff, and she was the most beautiful thing I'd ever seen.

In an act which has probably been replicated billions of times, in many different places, the newborn was gently put into the hands of its mother, and as I looked on, everything suddenly made sense to me, as I came to the realisation that moments such as this are moments that last forever, and everything was as it should be, simply because it was, and the mysteries of the universe could wait a while longer, because myself and Caroline now had a daughter. Caroline then asked me if I would like to hold my daughter, and I said yes, because to have said otherwise would have made absolutely no sense at all.

I held my daughter, fearful that I would let her fall, never realising that such a thing was impossible. For the rest of my life, or so the story goes, I would be someone who picked my daughter up after a fall: a make-things-better man who would be there to wipe a tear, and the man who would tell his daughter that, whatever happened, things would work out just fine, because she had a mother and father who would love her forever and ever, and in the end, that's really all that mattered. For a while, I would go away, but that is in the present, and no such place exists. But twelve years ago, as I looked down upon the face of my newborn daughter, my soul had told me that there could never be a greater love than this: a simple truth I will hold true until I draw my last breath.

I have decided not to attend my daughter's birthday party, because that's just the way things are, and in the present, some truths are still self-evident. Someday I will see my daughter again, but even though I am now sane, the time is not yet right. I love Jessica, and I know that Jessica loves me, but I'm taking my time, because sanity is something one should never take for granted.

The present which sits on the bar is invisible, shrouded as it is in paper that is white and pink and orange. I know nothing about the present. It might be small, it might be slightly larger than small, but I can't be sure. Kate Kowolski, the woman who is my neighbour and who might someday be my wife, went shopping on my behalf, and it is she who is responsible for the paper that is white and pink and orange.

Over a cup of coffee in her apartment, I had told my neighbour about my daughter's birthday party, and my neighbour had enquired into the status of the present I would be buying for my daughter. I told my neighbour that it was my intention to go shopping in search of a present for my twelve-year-old daughter just as soon as I could find out what it was that a twelve-year-old daughter would like. My neighbour then told me that perhaps the present my daughter would most like would be the presence of her father, and I told my neighbour that I couldn't go to the party because; and I didn't get beyond the bit about because, because that's just the way things were.

My neighbour didn't pursue the matter any further; she simply let things lie, which was probably for the best, and she went on to tell me about a gobshite she was dating called Gerald, who worked somewhere or other, doing something or other, and who she liked very much, because she just did. She never described Gerald as a gobshite in so many words, or in any amount of words, come to think of it, but I knew that he was a gobshite because some part of me wanted him to be a gobshite.

The conversation ended, and my neighbour returned to her apartment to sleep in oversized pyjamas, the colours of which were mostly mad.

Over a cup of coffee in my apartment the following evening (the gobshite was on a business trip to Hamburg, or some other place that was very far away), I told my neighbour about the present I had not bought. She enquired into the present that had not been bought, and I told her about the many shops which were to be found on Grafton Street and Henry Street and God knows where else, and how I had visited each and every one of them, in search of whatever it was that a twelve-year-old daughter would like, and how things didn't work out, because I was only a human being, and how I didn't know about twelve-year-old things in the world of today, because I wasn't twelve, and I finished by telling my neighbour that I was now a nervous wreck because I bloody well was.

Having listened to my perfectly rational explanation, my neighbour responded by throwing her eyes up to heaven, or the ceiling, or wherever. She then asked me for money. I didn't enquire as to why she wanted the money, because it would have been impolite and pointless, and anyway, I knew why she wanted the money, and within two or three seconds of her request, I had handed her the money, because that's just the way things were.

The following evening I sat at my kitchen table with my neighbour Kate Kowolski.

She told me that she hadn't time for a cup of coffee because she was going out to dinner with the gobshite who had returned from Hamburg, or some other place that was very far away, and as a result of this, there were no cups of coffee on the table, only a package that was coloured white and pink and orange. I asked her what was in the package, and she told me, and I thanked her, even if I'd never heard of it. She then proceeded to tell me about how she would have liked to hand over some change to me, but she went on to explain about how she couldn't, because the present she had purchased was very expensive. But that was of no consequence, she said, because it was my daughter's twelfth birthday, and she deserved the best of everything, My neighbour, who was a banker, then extorted some more money from me, as she told me once again how *very* expensive the present had been, and I handed over a cheque without complaint, because Jessica was my daughter, and nothing else mattered. My neighbour then left, and I found myself looking at a not-inexpensive present which was wrapped in paper that was white and pink and orange, and I knew that I would seriously have to get down to work on the novel which begins with the words 'There is a house', so that I could repay Caroline the money she'd lent me.

I hadn't asked Caroline to lend me any money, but she'd insisted, informing me that I could repay her just as soon as I got back on my feet. Caroline asked me how much money did I need to get back on my feet, and I told Caroline that I needed nothing, which was a lie, but I loved Caroline, and I still had my pride. Caroline then repeated her question, and I told the truth, informing her that I needed something slightly more than nothing, and Caroline proceeded to write a cheque for three times the something which was more than nothing, and I thanked Caroline, and she told me to be quiet, and I said nothing more.

Behind the bar the clock goes *tick-tock*, and it will soon be time for me to leave.

Caroline had rung me earlier this morning, and we arranged to meet outside a shop on Westmoreland Street, where I would hand over the package that was coloured white and pink and orange. I never rang Caroline at home, because she did not live alone, and I had not yet summoned up the courage to speak to the girl who was now twelve. In time I would, but not yet, for not yet is in the future, and some would say that no such place exists.

No, today I will stand outside a shop on Westmoreland Street and meet with the woman I still love, the woman I will always love, and I will ask her to deliver a package, which is something more than that: it is a message of love from a father to a daughter, a link between what was the past and what might yet be the future.

And elsewhere on Westmoreland Street, a man of my acquaintance will be smiling at passers-by, wearing a pair of sandals, and carrying the umbrella which he always carries with him.

20

It is now twelve years, two months and five days since my daughter was born, and I remain sane. The novel which will begin with the words 'There is a house' is going reasonably well, and page two will soon be passing on the baton to page three. The fact that page two has yet to receive the baton from page one is of little relevance, because these things take time, and the fifteen months, which became twelve months, which is now nine months, is quite a lot of time.

My daughter has yet to become reacquainted with her father, because that's just the way of things, I guess, and I will pick up the phone, or call to the house, or do whatever it is that I will end up doing, when I'm reasonably certain that the man she will meet is a man of whom she can be proud.

The way the story goes, there once was a man who lived with two women. He loved them, and they loved him. But gradually, over a period of time which probably stretched back as far back as he could remember, things started to go wrong for the man.

The way the story goes, he didn't play football because he couldn't play football, and he didn't dance because he couldn't dance. But then he became all grown up, and fell in love and started dancing. Mostly, he got by unaided, because that's what grown-ups do, but occasionally he would reach out for something beyond himself, and everything worked out just grand.

The days passed, and the grown-up became older and wiser and totally fucked up.

He used to reach out for the something that went beyond himself, so that he could dance, or fall in love, or do almost anything. But in time, he was to find himself reaching out for reasons which were quite beyond him, and this made him very unhappy. Things would have been made somewhat easier if he reached out every day, but the truth was that he would reach out only very occasionally, in reaction to a gentle breeze on a summer's day, or the simple fact that it was a Tuesday or a Wednesday or whatever.

He loved his daughter and she loved him. But sometimes the child would see her father fall over, or do something equally funny, and the child must have found this somewhat confusing.

The child's father and mother never got married. Twelve years, two months and five days ago, a child was born, and a love that had been shared between two now included another. The parents of the child did give some consideration to formalising their relationship, but no scrap of paper was needed to validate a love that was shared between a mother, a father, an infant, and a tomato called Domato, a land in which fairy tales were made real, and a time when they all lived happily ever after until, and for no reason in particular, the wheels fell off.

He remembers the day he told Caroline he was leaving. It was a Friday. She knew why he had to leave and she didn't try to stop him. He was mad and insane and all fucked up, and so he had decided that the time had now come for him to make his way through life elsewhere. There were many reasons why he had to leave, but the most important reason of all was asleep upstairs. No, Caroline didn't try to stop him from leaving; she still loved him, but the love that had existed once upon a time, when Valentine's cards had been exchanged, had long since gone, and in its place there was a genuine concern for the future of the man who was the father of her child.

As he left, Caroline suggested that he get help. He'd smiled at her when she'd suggested that. He knew, as did she. It was a Friday, which had nothing to do with anything in particular, but he was grand on that particular Friday, and because he was grand there was no need for help. Tomorrow, or the day after, it would be a different day to Friday, and he'd see what happened, which would probably be much the same as before.

He once wrote a book that sold very well, and so he bought himself an apartment which looked onto the River Liffey, and everything worked out for the best, or so the story goes.

21

The waiter looked like Des O'Connor, and he was wearing black shoes, black trousers, a white shirt and a black dicky bow.

Several hours earlier, I had sat at my kitchen table. A man was seated to the left of me.

It was Saturday morning, and Tom O'Brien was wearing jeans and a sweatshirt. A woman was seated to the right of me. It was Saturday morning, and Kate Kowolski was wearing trousers that could best be described as psychedelic, and a blouse that made her trousers seem quite boring in comparison.

I sat in my dressing gown, telling them both to go away.

'No,' I said.

'You'll like her,' he said.

'Feck off,' I said.

'It won't kill you,' she said.

'Not a chance,' I said.

'I'm paying,' he said.

'You are?' I said.

'I am,' he said.

'Yeah, well thanks for the offer, but I can't,' I said.

'You can't?' she said.

'No . . . I can't,' I said.

'Why?' he said.

'Because,' I said.

'Because what?' she said.

'Because,' I said.

'Because what?' Kate Kowolski asked me, although it was none of her business, and because she was my friend, she should have been supporting me, because that's what friends do; even if she was a friend who was dating a gobshite called Gerald. *Gerald?* What sort of name was that? I'd never met a Gerald who was anything other than a Gerald, and although I knew next to nothing about him, I had a clear picture of him in my mind, and I had to admire him for his courage in the way that he had come to terms with his buck-teeth and dandruff.

Because what? she had wanted to know. Because, Kate Kowolski, I do not want to go out to dinner with a woman called Claire, and the reason why I do not want to go out to dinner with a woman called Claire is because I am not ready to go out to dinner with a woman called Claire. I am sane now, Kate Kowolski, but I am, as yet, not ready. I hope I have made my position perfectly clear. Now please go away. Conversation over.

'Because what?' Kate Kowolski asked, again.

'Because,' I said, again.

I looked away from Kate Kowolski, not wishing to dwell on things. She had a determined look on her face, and in time, the decades of the future still to come, I will realise that there's just no beating Kate Kowolski when she has that look on her face. But for the moment she is a neighbour who is also a friend, and the circumstances which might lead to her someday becoming my wife have yet to occur, because that's just the way things are.

Silence descended for several seconds, and I lived in hope that my arguments had won the day. At some unspecified point in the future, I may well have enjoyed going out to dinner with a woman called Claire, who had a best friend called Suzanne, who had a partner called Tom O'Brien, but I had a book to write and I wanted Tom O'Brien and Kate Kowolski to go away and leave me in peace, because I just bloody well did.

'Paul, trust me, for you know I speak the truth. You *are* going out with me tonight,' Tom said. My hope that my argument had won the day was starting to fade somewhat, and I decided to change my tactics, which basically meant that I didn't know my arse from my elbow.

I looked at Tom O'Brien, the man who was my best friend and agent, and I knew that I was screwed. I then looked in the general direction of the woman who was dating a gobshite called Gerald, and I knew that I was similarly indisposed.

22

Tom O'Brien's nostrils lingered over the rim of his wineglass as Des O'Connor looked on. Other observers included Tom O'Brien's partner, Suzanne Charles, and her best friend, Claire Casey. There was one other observer present, but I didn't count, because I was Claire's date for the evening, and I was terrified.

Removing his nostrils from the rim of the wineglass, and using nimble fingers which had never seen a building site in their life, Tom O'Brien twirled the stem of the wineglass this way and that, and that way and this, as he began studiously to inspect its contents. Finally, sniffing and twirling now completed, Tom O'Brien supped from the glass, and as the liquid came in contact with his palate, he closed his eyes, and all was well.

Seconds later, and with his eyes now open, he pronounced his verdict on everything that had gone before.

'Excellent,' he informed Des O'Connor, and Des O'Connor was pleased.

Filling Tom O'Brien's wineglass to something approaching full, Des O'Connor then proceeded to do much the same with the wineglasses of Suzanne Charles and Claire Casey, before moving on to the wineglass which was in front of me, and I made a dog's bollix of things because I was sane, or so the story goes. According to the scheduling of these things, my wineglass was the last to be filled, but no such thing occurred, because no such wineglass was now on the table. In anticipation of the liquid to come, I had whipped the wineglass from its designated spot on the table and was now holding on to it, for no reason in particular, save for the fact that I wanted to keep my sanity intact.

Things weren't really as absurd as they might have first appeared, because I was to find myself explaining to a somewhat surprised Des O'Connor how everything made perfect sense.

'Fine, thanks . . . yeah, fine . . . don't drink . . . yeah, thanks,' I informed him.

Seemingly content with my explanation, Des O'Connor left our table, and if he looked back in my direction more than once, that was about the height of it.

'So, you, what are we working on?' Suzanne Charles, who was seated to the left of me, wanted to know what you, which was me, and we, which was also me, was working on. Simultaneously, she also removed the empty wineglass from my hand, and, replacing it on the table, she proceeded to fill it with water. I'm not really sure if Suzanne wanted to know what you, we, or me was working on, but in fairness to her, she was behaving as if nothing much had happened, and I was grateful to her, even if her attempt to retrieve a situation from the realms of the irretrievable was doomed to failure.

'Me? I'm . . . a novel. I'm working on a novel.' 'Paul, can you tell us anything about it?' Claire Casey wanted to know if I was in a position to discuss the page one which had yet to become page two, and I was grateful for the inquiry, because it put more distance between me and the dog's bollix that had occurred, when my sanity was high. Claire was seated opposite me, and she was about the same age as myself, and she was wearing a black skirt, a white blouse, and a black jacket with a slight tinge of blue. She was also smiling at me, which was something of a surprise, all things considered, and she seemed genuinely interested in eliciting a response to the question she had posed, which surprised me even more.

'It's . . . it's about a house, Claire.' 'A house?' Suzanne wanted to know.

'What kind of house?' my agent wanted to know, and I can't say I blamed him.

'An . . . old house,' his client informed him.

'How old?' my agent wanted to know.

'Old . . . very old,' I informed my agent.

'How old? Dublin Corporation old? Oliver Cromwell old? Define "old".' 'Well,' I went on to inform my agent, 'it's . . . ' 'It's none of our business what Paul's working on. Sorry, Paul, I shouldn't have asked you about the novel,' Claire said, still smiling at me.

'Claire, I *am* his agent. I don't think it's unreasonable if . . . ' 'Shut up, Tom. Claire is right. Don't worry, Paul will deliver and you'll get your 10 per cent.' Tom O'Brien's girlfriend had just told him to shut up, probably because she was a writer like myself, and she would have understood about houses which had yet to be built. She was also a client of Tom's, and she'd had some success, which was something that had eluded me since my first novel, but you don't really build houses hoping that they will last. You simply build them because you have to build them.

Tom had five writers under his wing, some successful, some less so, and I was his first, even if I did now fall into the category of the less so's.

Once upon a time I wrote a novel, and Tom handed the manuscript to a girl he was dating called Caitríona, and she handed it to her boss, and he published it. It sold very well, Tom became a literary agent, and such is life.

Myself and Suzanne had chowder for starters, Tom had the mushroom soup and Claire had the Caesar salad.

Claire told me that she was a nurse, and I asked her what kind of nurse, and she told me that she was a ward nurse in the Mater Hospital, which relieved me somewhat, because the Mater is not a psychiatric hospital, although I kept those thoughts to myself.

For the main course, I had the rack of lamb, Clare had the beef, Suzanne had something that looked strange, and Tom had the steak (rare), and then we all had ice cream for dessert, and the evening had lasted for three hours and fourteen minutes.

Between the three of them, my dinner companions had only consumed the one bottle of wine. I suspect that this might have had something to do with me, and I was disappointed if that was indeed the case, because I'm sure I would have handled things better the second time around.

At evening's end, my agent paid the bill, as promised. He also left a sizeable tip for Des O'Connor, and Des O'Connor was pleased. And if Des O'Connor looked at me more than once as we left the restaurant, that was about the height of it.

Outside, Tom suggested that we finish things off by going to a nightclub, but Claire said that even though she'd love to go to a nightclub, she couldn't, because she had to get up early for work the next morning. I didn't want to go to a nightclub, but I didn't know what to say, and so I repeated what Claire had said word for word, and Tom looked at me quite strangely. Tom then asked Suzanne if she fancied going to a nightclub, and Suzanne told Tom that he wasn't going anywhere, and so that was that.

Tom and Suzanne lived within walking distance of the restaurant, and Suzanne invited myself and Claire back for a coffee, but Claire passed, citing the reasons previously given, and I passed, giving much the same reasons.

We said our goodbyes, and Tom kissed Claire, and I kissed Suzanne, and Suzanne hugged Claire, and myself and Tom just nodded at each other, probably because he was my agent.

And so I ended up sharing a taxi with Claire.

Because the restaurant was on the southside, and Claire lived on the northside, the sharing of a taxi made sense, because I lived some place in between.

An adult, I sat in the back of the taxi with Claire as it crossed over Church Street Bridge. I had never met the girl before in my life, and yet I liked her very much, which seems a bit adolescent, but to say anything else would be a lie.

I loved Caroline; I always would. But we both knew that the love affair which had begun on Valentine's Day many years before had now ended, and that we were now on journeys which were exclusively our own. The past was the past, and there was no turning back. There simply was what there was: a present which would forever be shaped by the exchanging of envelopes which were white, and larger than normal, and which would ultimately lead to the birth of the child who was now twelve.

Few words were exchanged between myself and Claire as the taxi made its way towards Phibsboro, and I was relieved, because I was now sane, and absolutely terrified.

Eventually, the taxi pulled up outside a house somewhere close to the Mater Hospital, and Claire thanked me for a wonderful evening, which surprised me, and she then kissed me on the cheek, which surprised me even more. I then surprised myself by asking Claire if she fancied going out with me again, whenever, and Claire said that she would like that very much, and I said fine, and she said OK, and I said fine again. Claire then got out of the taxi, before getting back into the taxi again, the reason being, she said, that it might be a good idea if she gave me her phone number, and I agreed, because it did sound like a good idea. Claire then asked me if I had a pen, and I said no, but the taxi driver said he had a pen and a piece of paper if we were interested, and we said we were, and Claire proceeded to write down her home phone number, and the number of the hospital which was not psychiatric, on the piece of paper that the taxi driver had provided. Claire then got out of the taxi and walked towards the front door of the house in which she lived, and I asked the taxi driver if he wouldn't mind waiting until she had closed her front door after her, and he said grand. Claire then proceeded to open and close the front door after her, but not before smiling out at the taxi that had remained waiting, and the taxi driver smiled back at her, as did I.

I then headed off into the night with the taxi driver, spending the remainder of my journey looking at a piece of paper that had been handed to me, knowing that I would never make use of it, because even though I had asked Claire if she might fancy going out with me again, and notwithstanding the fact that she had replied in the affirmative, I knew that the question had been asked by someone other than myself: a strange creature who had momentarily believed that normality might be possible. But it did not take long for sanity to return, and the wallflower who was now sitting in the back seat with me whispered in my ear, telling me that I should get back in my box, and I obeyed, knowing that the wallflower always spoke the truth, or so the story goes.

23

Each night I dream, and each dream is the same, and that's just the way of things, I guess. Last night I dreamt of many things, including a soft drink which was notable for its absence. In an illusion brought on by sanity, I had put down that drink and replaced it with something stronger.

Each night I dream, and each dream brings my past into conflict with my present, and all is well, because my dream will involve the lifting of something other than a drink that is soft.

Subsequent to my visit to a restaurant, an occasion when sanity had run amok, I had succumbed to sleep and gone mad. Soft drink now absent, I stumbled upon people and places, as the ghosts of Christmas past, present and future had taken me in hand, and led me this way and that, that way and this, choreography totally absent.

I dreamed a dream, one of many dreams, each one of them the same. I saw a barman whistling 'Danny Boy', and I heard a communist talking about the equality of man. I saw the tears of a barber, and the smile of a man on Westmoreland Street. I saw myself looking on as two ducks fought over something or other, somewhere or other, and I saw the best friend who was seated beside me. I saw Man United playing Liverpool, and I saw the spectator who was standing elsewhere. I saw the neighbour who might someday be my wife looking after a man who had lost everything, and I saw the mother of my child heartbroken, as the man she once knew became something other.

Last night I dreamt of things, each one of them the same. But I did not see her, and she did not see me, and even though it was a dream, I was grateful. She is twelve, she is my daughter, and I love her. But whether it be in the world of dreams or reality, I think it best if she does not see the man who is her father, because she is deserving of someone better than me. Perhaps, in another time, another place, I will once again see my daughter, but that is in the future, and some would say that no such place exists.

Each night I dream, and each dream is the same, involving as it does chaos.

Each night I dream, and each dream is the same, and it is there that I find peace.

Today, the morning after the night before, I stare at my bedroom ceiling. On my bedside locker there is a piece of paper that contains a phone number, but I know that I will never make use of that phone number.

It is Sunday, and I have decided to write. Page two awaits, and I will become reacquainted with the world of words. Big words, small words. No big deal: just words.

Words permit me to become anyone, anywhere, but most importantly of all, they permit me to become something other than me.

Chapter 1 . . . The End, and something in between. There might be a prologue, but that doesn't count, because prologues are arrogant shites, remaining aloof from the main story, content to see what the words might reveal. I envy those prologues, because they usually know more than I do, which wouldn't be hard, considering I know feck all.

There is a house, I am told. Then what? There is a house and no story.

Words. Just words. Shite.

I have decided that page one will be a prologue, and

consequently that house will be looking on, awaiting news of its placement in the great scheme of things. Today I will start working on page two, and matters will be advanced, and everything will be grand, because I am a writer who is no longer blocked, because that's just the way things are.

Once, a long time ago, I lay down on a bed and put pen to paper. It was to be a short story: nothing too complicated. One year later, my short story had become a long story, and I was forever hooked, because that's what usually happens to people who accidentally find a drug of choice. I suspect that other addictions may lie elsewhere, but today is Sunday, and I will write because I am now sane.

And so, having decided to write, I mentally go through the pre-launch routine.

In order of importance, I check for:

Sanity	check
Cigarettes	check
Coffee	check
Inspiration	no

Three out of four ain't bad.

Turn on word processor. Plug in kettle. Fill my Italia '90 mug with spoonful of coffee and three sugars. Open fridge for milk. No milk. Where's the bloody milk? Shite. Can't drink black coffee. Don't like black coffee. Go to shop for milk? No, I'm still in my dressing gown. Get dressed? No, I'm in the zone. Thinking. Kate Kowolski. She'll have milk. Yes, open door, walk down corridor and ask Kate Kowolski for a drop of milk. She might still be asleep. It's 10 AM, but she'll understand.

Get a drop of milk and write. How difficult can it be?

24

At two minutes past ten o'clock, Kate Kowolski's doorbell rang. Several seconds later, and in response to the doorbell which had rung, Kate Kowolski opened her front door wearing pyjamas that were coloured green and purple and yellow, and she had an orange toothbrush sticking out of the side of her mouth. I said 'Good morning', and she mumbled something back at me, which I'm guessing was 'Good morning', but it's difficult to say, because the protruding toothbrush was obviously making dialogue difficult. She looked half-asleep, and a fair proportion of the left side of her face was covered by black hair which had yet to be brushed, and she looked quite beautiful.

As she turned away from her neighbour who was wearing a brown dressing gown, a verbal something or other that sounded like 'ciffee' was an indication to me that I should follow her. Closing the front door after me, I walked into her kitchen. A pot of coffee was brewing, and Kate Kowolski pointed in its general direction before heading towards her bathroom to finish the brushing of her teeth.

I proceeded to find myself a mug which had a picture of Elvis on it, and which exclaimed that he was the King, because he probably was. I had started to pour myself a coffee, the standard of which was quite beyond me, or so I was once told, when I stopped my pouring in response to a sound I heard coming from the general direction of Kate Kowolski's bedroom. It was a whistling sound, and so I quickly found myself coming to the conclusion that somebody was whistling. Elsewhere, I could hear a gargling sound coming from Kate Kowolski's bathroom, but that held little interest for me, because the urgle-urgle-urgle that was occurring elsewhere was only to be expected.

No, I did not dwell on happenings elsewhere, because happenings elsewhere were not at the races when compared to the sound of a man's whistling. I knew that it was a man, because I'm a writer, and writers know these things. But who was this man and what was he whistling? I listened very carefully, but it was difficult to make out. I knew that it wasn't 'Danny Boy', so that ruled out Jim the barman. It sounded like something from U2, although it could just as easily have been something from Daniel O'Donnell.

So, there was a man in Kate Kowolski's bedroom. When she had stopped gargling, should I tell her about it? It might, after all, be a burglar who liked U2-stroke-Daniel O'Donnell. Perhaps there was no need to tell Kate Kowolski about the man who was in her bedroom. If the man was her father, or her brother, or her cousin or something, I'm quite sure that Kate Kowolski would have been only too well aware of the fact that they'd been her guest for the night. There was one other possibility that went beyond burglars and relatives, but I dismissed it out of hand, because I just did.

I finished pouring my coffee at about the same time that Kate Kowolski finished her urgle-urgling, and she returned to the kitchen, toothbrush now absent.

'So?' she asked me, as she proceeded to pour herself a mug of coffee. Her mug was much the same as mine, except for the fact that it made no reference to Elvis or royalty, opting instead to inform anyone who was interested that the Tower of London was in London, which must have seemed pretty original at the time.

'So?' I replied, still listening to the whistling which seemed to have moved on from U2-stroke-Daniel O'Donnell, opting instead to mimic whatever song came twenty-third in any Eurovision Song Contest you care to mention.

'Last night. How did it go?' 'Last night went . . . fine,' I said, being sure to smile as I lied, because I still had some modicum of pride left.

'That bad, huh?' 'Yes, Kate, it was that bad,' I said, being sure not to smile as I told the truth, because I just couldn't.

'Paul Conroy, what are we going to do with you?' 'Well, you could start by giving me a jug of milk.' 'Writing today?' 'Yeah, why not?' 'It's as good a day as any. So, tell me about last night.' The conversation that was taking place between myself and my neighbour Kate Kowolski was a conversation which was accompanied by a constant whistling noise, and Kate Kowolski would have had to be deaf not to have heard it, but she made no reference to same, and this told me that her apartment was not being burgled. In truth, I was relieved, because I was only wearing a pair of slippers, a pair of pyjamas, and a brown dressing gown, and the pursuit which would surely have followed would have been severely compromised, due to the fact that I would have looked quite ridiculous running down the quays in clothing that was not suited.

Having removed a burglar from the equation, I sat down at my neighbour's kitchen table and proceeded to tell her about the events which had occurred the previous evening, although I didn't get very far, and the reason I didn't get very far was because my neighbour's bedroom door opened, and the man who was her father, or brother, or cousin, or whatever, made his appearance. He smiled at me, and I smiled at him, and he kept smiling at me, and so I kept smiling at him. I also found myself coming to the conclusion that he was not Kate Kowolski's father, because he was about the same age as myself, and he hadn't got buck-teeth or dandruff, although that's got nothing to do with anything.

The man who was Kate Kowolski's brother, or cousin or something, walked to the table and kissed his sister-stroke-cousin on the top of her head, which was none of my business, but there you have it. Kate Kowolski then kissed her brother-stroke-cousin on the side of the cheek, and one and one suddenly made three: a mathematical equation which was confirmed when Kate Kowolski made the introductions.

'Paul, I'd like you to meet Gerald the gobshite,' she said, although admittedly she didn't actually refer to Gerald as a gobshite, which was for the best, I suppose.

'Paul Conroy, I'm very pleased to meet you. I couldn't believe it when Kate told me that the two of you were neighbours. I've just finished reading *Goodbye to Tomorrow*, and I have to say I thought it was superb.' 'Em . . . thank you,' I said. Gerald the gobshite was not only a gobshite, he was also a liar. The chances of me bumping into one of my readers were slim, bordering on non-existent, and I was only too well aware of the fact that Gerald the gobshite was using me as a way of ingratiating himself with my neighbour Kate Kowolski, and I know this because I'm a writer, and I wasn't born yesterday.

'Could you do me one small favour?' Gerald the gobshite and liar wanted me to do him one small favour, and he could go to hell, as far as I was concerned.

'Certainly,' I replied.

'If I left my copy with Kate, would you sign it for me?' Gerald the gobshite and liar, who had quite clearly never read anything written by me in his life, would make a point of going into Eason's tomorrow with the sole intended purpose of buying a copy of my latest book and, purchase completed, he would pass it on to Kate Kowolski, who would pass it on to me. It was disgraceful, bordering on obnoxious, but a sale's a sale.

'It would be my pleasure,' I said, because there was nothing much else I could say.

I was then to spend the next hour sitting at a kitchen table with Kate Kowolski and the man who was not related to her, and I was to find myself answering question after question about the this-and-thats of my latest book, each question asked by the man who was a gobshite and liar, and who was hanging on my every word, as I did my best to elaborate on the intricacies of plot and character motivation, and everything else that a writer is supposed to know about.

To his credit, Gerald the gobshite and liar had obviously read the jacket of *Goodbye to Tomorrow*, and it must have been pretty informative, because he seemed to understand the book fairly well. Many of the questions I could not answer, because sometimes a writer is the last person to understand, but we keep that secret to ourselves, opting instead for conversations couched in allusion, or so the story goes.

Questions asked, questions answered, Kate Kowolski returned to the events of the night before, but I did not want to go there, because Gerald the gobshite was sitting at the table, and I still had some modicum of pride left, and so I told them everything, including the bit about the wine bottle from hell.

Gerald the gobshite smiled at me when I mentioned the wine bottle from hell, and it was easy for him to smile, because he could not understand. I had made a dog's bollix of something, and I alone knew the wallflower who had sat in a restaurant, on a night when sanity had run riot.

Ten o'clock in the morning had now become eleven o'clock in the morning, and, having discussed almost everything that there was to discuss, I got up from the table to leave.

As I walked to the front door of my neighbour's apartment, Kate Kowolski reminded me about the reason for my visit, but I passed on her offer of a jug of milk, because I would start working on page two tomorrow.

Stepping onto the landing which had once been the location for a book signing, Gerald the gobshite stepped out with me, which was something of a surprise.

He said goodbye, although he didn't say goodbye exactly. What he had to say was strange, bordering on mad.

'Paul, you know you don't *have* to drink,' was his farewell to me, which seemed a bit strange, but there you have it.

'Gerald, I'm not drinking,' was my truthful reply to the statement that was strange, bordering on mad.

Gerald the gobshite smiled at me, and as I looked into his eyes, I recognised that smile.

It was a smile of someone who knew about wallflowers and things, but most importantly of all, it was a smile of someone who understood. I wasn't quite sure how it had come to pass that Gerald the gobshite could have understood, but it was quite apparent to me that he did.

Two wallflowers on the same landing, and one of them was smiling.

The other wallflower wasn't crying exactly, he was just being what he was: and what he was was all he could ever be, or so the story goes.

25

I went into a restaurant and made a dog's bollix of things. It was a Saturday. The following day was Sunday, and the day following that was Monday, which was yesterday, because it was now Tuesday.

I stand surrounded. To the left of me there is a man who is an expert on Spike Milligan.

He is writing a biography of Spike because Spike is now dead, and besides, Spike had always told us that he was ill. Spike was a tortured genius – that's what the expert on Spike Milligan tells me. The man who is an expert on the life of Spike is a retired schoolteacher who liked Spike; he didn't think he was funny, but he liked him. I ask the retired schoolteacher why he is writing a biography about Spike if he didn't think he was funny. He replies by telling me that he knew Spike was funny, but he didn't think he was funny as in funny-funny. I then ask the retired schoolteacher to give me an example of funny-funny, and he tells me that Jimmy Tarbuck is funny-funny.

Spike once wrote a poem about a goldfish. It was called 'My Wet Pet'. The poem had one line, and three words, and those three words were: 'My wet pet'. I asked the expert on Spike if he thought this was funny, and he said no, and I said nothing, because Spike probably wouldn't have wanted me to say anything.

The retired schoolteacher who is cataloguing the life of

Spike is writing a book about a tortured genius, but I'm not sure if Spike would have been that bothered about reading the book that is being written about him, because Spike once wrote a poem called 'My Wet Pet', and besides, Spike always told us that he was ill.

I stand surrounded. I am at a book launch in the Central Hotel, and the book that is being launched is called *Arrighan and Valentine*. It is a love story, and it was written by a woman called Marita Lavelle. It is the first book she ever wrote, and because I also once wrote a book for the first time, I wanted to be present, so that I could witness the most important night in someone's life.

Yesterday, two days on from the wine bottle from hell, I received some post. It was from my publishers, inviting me to the book launch.

Sanity returned, social skills now functioning at something near something, I decided to accept the invitation that had been sent to me, and so I rang Tom and asked him if he would like to go to the book launch with me, and he said no. I then asked him why he wouldn't go to the book launch with me, and he said that Suzanne was launching the book, and consequently he wanted to go with her, which made some sort of sense. I then asked him if I could go to the book launch with himself and Suzanne, and he said no, and I asked him why, and he then made reference to a friend of Suzanne's called Claire, by telling me that Suzanne had told him that Claire had told her about the passing on of a phone number, and he then suggested to me that I should make use of that phone number.

Because I'm a writer, I know about these things, and I realised that Tom was a best friend who was simply trying to improve my social life, and so I asked him once more if I could go to the book launch with himself and Suzanne, and he told me to ring Claire, and I said nothing, because there was nothing I could say.

I spent most of yesterday going for a walk, because I figured there was little else I could do. I'd spoken to Tom, and he'd reminded me about a woman called Claire, and I knew that I would never ring her, and I needed some fresh air.

And so I left my apartment and walked down the quays. Hanging a left down Capel Street, a subsequent right found me walking down Jervis Street, before I eventually made my way onto O'Connell Street, with Henry Street coming someplace in between.

I also visited the occasional bookshop or two, checking out the latest best-sellers, and doing something I would occasionally do, which might seem a bit sad, but a sale's a sale: upon entering a bookshop, I would start to behave like a normal customer and, placing an index finger in contact with my lower lip, I would peruse the various shelves that were home to books about this, that and everything else, before arriving at a location which was nowhere near that week's best-sellers. Then, gradually and unnoticed, I would bend down, always being careful to avoid the slipping of a disc, and then, taking a book from which ever shelf was closest to the floor, I would slowly stand up again, before reading the blurb which was on the back of my chosen book: a blurb which was accompanied by a picture of the author, a portrait which would have done justice to Brian Keenan once upon a time in Beirut.

A sale's a sale, and because pride has no place in a sale, I would do what usually came next: still perusing the blurb, I would slowly walk towards the shelves which contained that week's best-sellers, and, having arrived at my destination, I would linger for several seconds, before deciding that *Goodbye to Tomorrow* was not the book for me. My decision made, I would then put the copy of my unsold book on a shelf, leaving it nestling side by side with books that were probably overrated or, even if they weren't, should have been.

Yesterday I went for a walk. Book promoted, I crossed over O'Connell Street, passing people who were building a something or other, which was apparently going to replace a something or other that had once been blown up, because that's just the way of things, I guess. I'm not sure what the new something or other is supposed to represent, but I've seen the plans, and I've little doubt that all other syringes will pale in comparison.

Walk completed, I sat at a bar. Still sane, I drank a cup of coffee. Behind the bar, the clock went *tick-tock*.

Looking into the mirror which was situated behind the bar, Brian Keenan looked back at me. Beside him sat a communist who sold the occasional pack of twenty. Beside the communist sat a barber who's been on a lunch break which is never-ending, consequent to once upon a time when personal holocausts were ignored. Perhaps they are still being ignored; difficult to say. But in time, time will reveal all, because it always does, but sometimes it's too late.

Lips contorted, 'Danny Boy' flirted with the surrounding ether, and all was as it should have been.

I drank coffee, because I was still sane, but I did not dwell in front of the mirror too long, for fear that something other than my current state of mind might return.

I was big and strong and all grown up, and so I left my friends, heading home to an apartment which contained a phone number that would never be rung.

He smiled at me as I crossed over Westmoreland Street, and I smiled back, because he was a nice man, and he deserved a smile.

26

I stand surrounded. To the left of me stands Spike Milligan's greatest admirer. In front of me stands a man who grew up in Cork city many years ago, and who had fifteen brothers and twenty-six sisters, all of whom had to share a small bed with their mother, father, two grandmothers and two grandfathers. One of the grandfathers died, or so the story goes, but they didn't bury him; they simply repackaged him and sold his spare parts to neighbours who couldn't afford to buy firewood, and the man who is now standing in front of me grew up and bought the franchise for a Japanese motorbike something or other, and became rich, and wrote his autobiography, and it went on to sell a lot of copies in Cork and other places, or so I was told. In truth, I never read his book, because I just didn't, and I'm a real writer, not like him, and jealousy plays absolutely no hand, act or part in it.

The man who grew up in Cork stands in front of me saying little, which is probably just as well, because I doubt if I could understand the accent he has brought with him since childhood.

I stand surrounded. To the right of me stands P. J. Ryan. An author like myself, we usually end up fighting tooth and nail for that coveted spot on the bottom shelf, and I usually win out, through sheer, natural talent. P.J. doesn't say much, which isn't that unusual for an author. Several minutes earlier we had ended up standing side by side, and he asked me how the writing was coming along, and I said fine, and he smiled at me because he understood.

I stand surrounded by a retired schoolteacher, a Corkman who once wrote a book, and an author – although P.J. wasn't really surrounding me, because he keeps to himself mostly. My three companions all had a drink in their hands, unlike me, who had nothing in my hands, and the reason I had nothing in my hands is because the woman I would never ring had left our company in pursuit of a drink for myself and herself.

I didn't go to the book launch alone, because I rang the woman I would never ring, and everything worked out just grand, because I was now sane, or so the story goes.

27

Yesterday, bookshops visited, old friendships renewed, I crossed over O'Connell Street Bridge and walked on the River Liffey.

Those who know about these things tell us that Dublin is not in Dublin, located as it is on the outskirts of Paris, and consequently some gobshite had built a boardwalk adjacent to one of the quaysides, and such is life.

On that boardwalk there is a small café, and I rested there for a moment, keeping company with a soft drink and a chocolate éclair. Behind me, no more than three feet away, articulated lorries trundled past en route to the Continent, which seemed a bit silly, seeing as how they were already there, but I didn't complicate things by thinking too much about them, preferring instead to watch a river go by.

I sat on a boardwalk, not thinking too much, because I thought it was for the best. In time, I would see my daughter again, because I love her, and I found myself remembering the fairy tales, and a tomato called Domato.

I looked at the river, and I remembered the day Valentine's cards were exchanged, and how Caroline had read aloud the verse which was written on the card I had sent her; only it wasn't my card, belonging as it did to another – until it turned out that the other was me.

I looked at the river, not thinking too much about a lot of things, and I knew that I would never ring Claire Casey, a nurse who didn't work in a psychiatric hospital, and I told myself that it was for the best.

Sanity is transient, and the breeze that was blowing down from the Ha'penny Bridge was a reminder to me that one should never eat a chocolate éclair whilst sitting above a river, especially when the trousers you are wearing are not black in colour, but that has feck all to do with sanity, and I wasn't really sure what did.

I looked at the river, not thinking too much, and I decided to ring Claire Casey, a nurse who didn't work in a psychiatric hospital.

28

I left the boardwalk and returned to my apartment. I then made myself a cup of coffee and smoked three cigarettes. I then made myself another cup of coffee and smoked three more cigarettes. I then made a phone call, and it went something like this.

'Hello, is that the Mater Hospital? . . . Hi . . . Yeah, could I speak to Claire Casey, please . . . A nurse . . . She's a nurse . . . Not sure exactly, but she's not a psych – Sorry, no . . . Not sure . . . Yeah, I'll hold . . . Thanks . . . ' (Next two minutes spent listening to boy band who should be shot, which wouldn't be the worst thing in the world, considering that I'm on to a hospital. They seem to be singing about a girl who, it would seem, is the most important thing that ever happened to them. Why this should be, I'm not sure. It's a hospital, so perhaps she's a midwife.

You're the most important thing that's ever . . . Paul? Yes? Stop singing. I wasn't singing. You were. Wasn't. Was. Wasn't. Who *is* this girl? Does she know she has so many admirers? Does she care? Has she ever listened to them singing? *You're the most* . . . Shut up. Sorry. Could I suggest something? Yes. It might be a good idea if you ran through whatever in hell it is you're going to say to Claire Casey when she answers the phone. You think? I do. But what will I say? How in hell do I know? It was your idea. It was? It was. OK, how about: 'Hi, Claire, it's me . . . Paul . . . ah, so you remember? I'd heard that you were hoping I might ring, so I just thought . . . No, honestly, Claire, it was nothing . . . No, really . . . Tonight? Sorry, Claire. I know you must fancy me to bits, and I can understand your impatience, but I was thinking that we might get together tomorrow night . . . You would? Excellent. Tomorrow night it is.' How did that sound? Excellent, you'll have her eating out of your hand. You think? Absolutely. *You're the most important . . .*) Shite! Boy band over.

Phone answered.

Shite. Burned tip of finger with cigarette. Shite.

'Hello, could . . . could I speak to Claire Casey please?' 'Claire . . . It's you . . . I mean, you answered the phone . . . I mean, it's me . . . Hello.' Claire then said something sane, which I mostly forget, because I just do, and I continued on much as before, which was quite similar to almost everything that followed.

'Erm . . . I'm at home. And you? Well, I know that you're not at home because I've just rung you at work, which means that you're working, I guess. How . . . what do you do? . . . I mean, I know that you're a nurse thing . . . but what sort of . . . ' Claire then stepped in again, and said something sane which made some sort of reference to her nurse thing, and I did what I did.

'Intensive care? That must be pretty . . . serious?' Claire, who still hadn't hung up, then went on to tell me that Intensive Care was pretty serious, and I sucked the tip of my finger because it was sore.

'Erm . . . tomorrow night, Claire . . . I was wondering . . . Erm, there's this thing . . . a book launch . . . I was wondering . . . I was . . . ' Claire then said something which surprised me, all things considered, and I responded to her, everything about me a picture of perfect sanity.

'You would? . . . Erm, great . . . Yeah . . . erm . . . yeah . . . great . . . Tomorrow . . . Right . . . Bye . . . ' The conversation should have ended there and then, but Claire said something which, on the face of it, made sense, and so I continued with the conversation.

'I didn't? Sorry, it's in the Central Hotel at eight o'clock . . . Er, do you fancy meeting . . . meeting for a drink beforehand . . . I mean, you can drink and I . . . ' Claire then informed me that she would like to meet me for a drink beforehand.

'Long Hall? Yeah, OK. . . . Seven thirty . . . Great . . . See you then.' Claire then informed me that she was looking forward to it, 'it' being hard to define exactly, but I found it difficult to believe that 'it' could be me.

'Bye.' Conversation over, I hung up and sucked my finger because it was sore. I then spent the next couple of minutes, or hours, or whatever, going over our telephone conversation in my head, but I was finding it somewhat difficult, because my head was up my arse.

29

I stand, awaiting rescue, surrounded by three people who have little to say for themselves, and I am quite comfortable with my surroundings, because conversation does not come easily to a man who is now sane.

To the left of me stands the man who can tell the difference between funny and funny-funny. To the right of me stands a fellow author: a man who keeps his thoughts to himself, except for those moments when they find themselves liberated by the words which exist within his books. In front of me stands a Corkman who once wrote a book, although he isn't really a writer, because his book sold too well, and that's just that.

I stand, awaiting rescue, and several minutes after she volunteered to go to the bar for drinks, my rescuer returns, carrying a soft drink and a glass of wine.

Because it was the most important night in the life of Marita Lavelle, her publishers had decreed that there would be a free bar, and because the Library Bar in the Central Hotel contained several writers, the free bar was in danger of running dry soon after it opened.

Earlier that evening I had met Claire outside the Long Hall at seven thirty, although I'd arrived at seven fifteen, just to be sure. We had one drink each, and I kept my sanity by sticking with my usual, which was forever to be, or so the story goes, a soft drink, and because sanity wasn't that big an issue with Claire, she had a gin and tonic, and it smelt gorgeous.

We talked about this, that and Tom, and Claire was wearing a pinstriped jacket, which was complemented by a white blouse, and a skirt that was cream, although some would say that it was more brown than cream – but I couldn't be sure, because I'm a man – and she looked gorgeous.

We then walked the couple of hundred yards down to the Central Hotel and made our way up to the Library Bar on the first floor – the place where a writer called Marita Lavelle would experience something that was unlike anything that had ever gone before.

As we entered the bar, our arrival was noted by Audrey Harrigan, a person who had two roles to play in my life, neither of which could have been easy, but she carried out her duties of publicist and personal psychiatrist without complaint. In the weeks leading up to the launch of one of my books, Audrey would ease the inevitable tension which would be boiling up inside me by telling me that everything would be grand, or by the issuing of a kick up the backside, or by the doing of both at the same time, and she usually managed to calm me down, because she'd worked with a lot of writers, and she'd once told me that she knew what made writers tick, although she'd never made any actual reference to insanity.

Audrey said hello to me, and I introduced Audrey to Claire. My publicist and personal psychiatrist then positioned herself between me and Claire and, taking us by the arm, led us towards a corner of the bar. Three people were standing in that corner, and upon my arrival the first thing I noticed was the silence, and I correctly came to the conclusion that the absence of dialogue was a direct result of the absence of conversation. Audrey clearly must have been hoping that my presence in their midst might have livened things up somewhat, although alternatively, she may well have written the threesome off as a lost cause, and decided to make the lost cause a foursome.

This might possibly explain why Audrey suggested to Claire that she should accompany her to the bar, although it was just as likely that she wanted to make use of an opportunity that had presented itself to her, and the opportunity that had presented itself to Audrey was an opportunity to get to know the woman who was new in my life.

Audrey had left university several years ago and joined the publishing house I now called home. The first book she ever worked on was my first book, and we'd worked together ever since. We were good friends, and she knew nearly everything that there was to know about me, but she couldn't have known about Claire, because even I hadn't known about Claire until a few days previously.

And so it was that, some time later, my rescuer returned with two drinks. Claire hadn't had the opportunity to ask me what I was drinking earlier, hijacked as she was by Audrey, but she correctly assumed that I was sane, handing me as she did a soft drink.

I made the introductions, starting with P.J., who smiled and blushed at Claire, as was his way, before moving on to the man from Cork, who said something that sounded like a greeting, although I couldn't be entirely certain, and I finished by introducing Claire to the man who knew Spike Milligan better than Spike knew himself.

Introductions made, I then decided to become the centre of attention by talking about the weather, and I was just about to open my mouth and begin to say whatever it was I was going to say when I was beaten to the punch by Spike

Milligan's biographer, who asked Claire if she liked Spike Milligan.

Question asked, I stole a glance at P.J., who stole a glance at me, and we both knew that Spike Milligan was once again to be discussed till God knew when. The man from Cork didn't steal a glance at anyone, because he just didn't.

Claire informed Spike Milligan's biographer that she liked Spike Milligan very much, and that was that, or so myself and P.J. hoped. The man from Cork didn't seem too bothered either way.

Elsewhere in the room, I could see that Tom and Suzanne had arrived. Suzanne waved over in our direction, and Claire waved back, and I waved too, not wishing to be rude. Suzanne then pointed to her watch, indicating that she'd join us as soon as she could. I knew that Suzanne had a job to do, and the launching of a book – any book – is something that should be done with care and attention. But when that book is a first book, Suzanne would have known that the job in hand went beyond what might normally have been expected, and consequently she spent each and every minute prior to the launch in the company of the person who would soon become an author, promising her that everything would work out just fine.

Tom O'Brien had been in the room no more than a minute when he started to do what, by necessity, he always had to do. An author's agent, he would spend the evening saying hello to everyone and anyone, networking the room, never knowing what the simplest of conversations could lead to.

'Nice weather we're having,' I didn't say to Claire. I was going to, but I never got the chance, cut off at the pass as I was by someone who was in our company.

Claire had been asked if she liked Spike Milligan by the

someone who was in our company, and she had replied by saying yes, she liked Spike Milligan very much. As far as myself and P.J. were concerned (the man from Cork didn't seem that bothered either way), that was an end to it; the life and times of Spike Milligan had been covered, and we could now move on to the weather, because great and all as Spike had been, there was only so much Spike that myself and P.J. could take in a single lifetime.

However, it turned out that myself and P.J. were wrong, because we were writers, and we knew about these things.

'But do you not think he was a bit . . . tortured?' the person in our company proceeded to ask Claire.

I looked at Claire and I could see that she was giving the matter some thought. P.J. looked at Claire, probably thinking something similar. The man from Cork was thinking about a dead grandfather.

'Tortured?' Claire asked. ' Well . . . ' Claire said, before continuing with her analysis of Spike. 'I *would* say that Spike was a manic depressive who had achieved a great insight into himself,' Claire said, finishing her analysis of Spike.

'Those are my thoughts *exactly*,' the person in our company said, agreeing with Claire.

'But . . . ' Claire said, continuing with her analysis of Spike, 'I would also have to say that, whilst it is true that much of his greatness was derived from his depression, he could be, and usually was, funny. You see, I think he understood about the absurdity and magnificence which often combine to create the human condition. But ultimately, I think that his greatest legacy must surely be his laughter; laughter at himself, and laughter at us, quite simply because he *was* one of us,' Claire said, finishing her analysis of Spike.

And that was that. Claire had given her tuppence-worth on the life of Spike Milligan, and there could be little more for saying; little more that could be said.

I looked at P.J., and P.J. looked at me, and we both knew that the matter was now closed. I could see by the look on the face of Spike's biographer that the matter was also now closed as far as he was concerned, even if it was only for a minute or two. I looked at the man from Cork, and I could see that he was elsewhere, probably reflecting on a poverty-stricken childhood spent in Cork: the time when to have had three in a bed was considered to be the lap of luxury.

But something strange had happened while Claire was discussing the life of the comic genius who once wrote a poem called 'My Wet Pet'. Because as she spoke, a smile never leaving her face, I felt her left hand leaning on my right arm.

Now, she could well have been leaning on my right arm for support – the bar was free after all, and who knows how many drinks she might have had before returning to me – but somehow I doubted it. In all probability, the reason she had placed her left hand on my right shoulder was simply because she did, but I didn't think about it a whole lot, because I just didn't.

I was about to start up a conversation about something or other, probably the weather, when a loud voice asked everyone in the room to be quiet. Obeying its command, my gaze followed the gaze of everyone else, and I focused my attention on the centre of the room.

Tom Collins – the man who had been my publisher since once upon a time in the beginning, and the person who had now taken Marita Lavelle under his wing – was standing centre stage. Beside him stood Suzanne, and beside her stood the woman who was about to see the most wonderful of dreams come true.

I knew little about Marita Lavelle. She looked to be about

the same age as I was when my own dream had come true, but the one thing I knew with absolute certainty was that soon, in a matter of moments, Marita Lavelle was someone who would forever be a novelist. Perhaps her book was to be the first of many books; perhaps it would be her only book. Either way, it didn't really matter, because Marita Lavelle had written the most important book of all, and in time she would come to realise, if she didn't know it already, that what she'd achieved was something that could never be taken away from her.

My publisher made a brief speech, congratulating Marita on her achievement, and he then handed over to Suzanne, who had a singular task to perform, becoming as she did the midwife who was introducing a newborn into the world of books. She told us about how honoured she was to be the one who was launching Marita's book, and how that book was quite magnificent, and as she spoke I looked at Marita, and written across her face I saw the terror of someone who was now entering the unknown. But as I looked at the faces of the family and friends who were standing beside Marita, I saw no terror, only pride, and the occasional tear.

Suzanne finished by informing the universe and beyond that Marita's book was now launched, and those present, and those who had gone before us, applauded.

And then, her voice trembling, Marita proceeded to read the opening lines of her book, and as she read, the trembling receded, and Marita took full possession of what was hers, and because it was hers, she now had to give it away, because that's just the way of things.

Book launched, myself and Claire stood in a long line of people who were queuing up to buy a copy of the latest addition to the world of the imagination: a list which probably stretches back to a once upon a time when a temperamental caveman looked at the blank wall which stood in front of him. Chalk in hand, he would have begun to work on a first draft and, first draft completed, he would have knocked down the wall and begun to work on a second draft and, second draft completed, he would have delivered the completed work to his publisher, who would have rejected it, because the wall was either too big, too small, too deep, too shallow, or too something in between, and the caveman would then do the only thing he could do, which was to find a new wall elsewhere, and do whatever came next, because to have done otherwise would have made no sense at all.

Purchases completed, Claire then handed her copy of the book to its creator, and following on from instructions received, Marita Lavelle signed her name, but not before writing a note in which she passed on the warmest of regards to Claire Casey.

I then handed my copy to the woman who was now a fellow author, and following on from yet more instructions received, Marita Lavelle signed my copy, but not before passing on her warmest regards to a person called Jessica. How it came to pass that a person called Jessica had entered into the equation is difficult to say, although it's probably something to do with the fact that she's my daughter and I love her.

I then shook hands with Marita and said well done, and she thanked me, and I said that it was me who should be thanking her.

Myself and Claire then found ourselves in the company of Suzanne, and we both congratulated her on a job well done. Suzanne thanked us, and then made reference to the fact that I had rung Claire, and I said nothing, because I think I was embarrassed.

The evening ended with me being waylaid by Tom Collins, the man who is my publisher. A lover of books, he has been producing them for three decades, and he once told me that he thinks people who make books, both authors and publishers, are damned lucky, which kinda makes sense.

I introduced him to Claire, and he asked her if she'd enjoyed the evening, and she said that yes, she really had. He then turned his attention to me, which always made me nervous, and he asked me how the new book was coming along, and I said fine, and he then asked me what it was about, and Claire told him that it was about a house, and he looked at Claire and smiled.

Book launch over, Marita Lavelle's life forever changed, I walked out into Exchequer Street with Clare, Suzanne and Tom, who by this time had finished networking everyone and anything that moved, and the four of us headed off towards no place in particular.

Once, several months previously, I had had occasion to walk down that same Exchequer Street, but that was then, and now is now, and I am sane.

30

Walking side by side, Claire and Suzanne slowly made their way down Suffolk Street, talking about whatever it is that women talk about as they slowly make their way down Suffolk Street. Following closely behind, Tom and I talked about whatever it is that men talk about as they slowly make their way down Suffolk Street.

We had a fine chat: nothing too complicated.

'Grand evening,' Tom said, discussing the weather, and nothing much else.

'It is,' I said, agreeing with Tom about the current state of the weather, because it was indeed a grand evening, and so it seemed like the right thing to say.

'Paul?' Tom said, in a voice that was unusually subdued, and I got the distinct impression that Tom wanted to steer our conversation away from the weather and move it on elsewhere. To where exactly was difficult to say, but Tom's demeanour told me that elsewhere was a place that contained several things, most notably awkwardness and embarrassment for the man who was my best friend.

'Yes, Tom?' I said, replying to the voice that had gone before. My tone was also subdued, because it usually was, and besides, having done the mental arithmetic, the maths told me that there was only one topic that could possibly have been responsible for causing so much angst for Tom, and I would have much preferred it if he did the the decent thing and avoided discussing my body odour. As far as I was aware, my body odour was pretty much odourless, but because I was a writer who knew about life, I was only too well aware of the fact that those whose bodies are not odourless are often the last to know.

'Paul, I've been thinking.' Tom, it turned out, had been thinking. He had also been smelling, but I suppose that 'Paul, I've been smelling' wouldn't have made much sense.

'You have?' 'I have.' 'Thinking about what, Tom?' 'Oh, nothing in particular,' Tom said, clarifying the position perfectly.

'OK,' I said, and I was more than happy to leave things as they were, remembering as I did a tone of voice that had hinted at smelling.

Three or four seconds later, Tom returned to the subject of smelling.

'Paul?' 'Yes, Tom?' 'I . . . I've something I want to say to you, and it's . . . difficult.' Tom had just told me that he was finding it difficult to casually bring up the subject of my body odour, which seemed fair enough. In front of us, Claire and Suzanne had crossed the street and were turning up Grafton Street. Tom and I waited for a 46A bus to pass before crossing the road in pursuit of two women who had never stopped talking about whatever it is that women talk about whenever they turn onto Grafton Street. Following in their footsteps, I was accompanied by Tom and a God-awful stench, and because I was a writer who knew about life, I decided to cop myself on and come to terms with reality. I did not suffer from body odour. I knew this because I just bloody well did. No, body odour had taken a hike. I considered the options and immediately came to the conclusion that Tom wanted to discuss my bad breath. But I didn't have bad breath. *Did* I have bad breath? Did I have bad breath *and* body odour? Shite.

Tom had said that he had something difficult to say to me. The fact that he hadn't spoken since told me that my body odour and bad breath must have been pretty serious.

Still, I was a man who was a grown-up, and so I decided to make things easy for my best friend by saying something, although it wasn't exactly profound.

'Tom, what is it that you want to say to me?' was the thing I said, not looking in Tom's direction as I did so, for fear that the stench of my bad breath might knock him out. And as for the body odour? I suppose I could always have walked on the other side of Grafton Street, even if that would have made conversation somewhat difficult. But I calculated that a distant conversation which was bereft of odour was preferable to one that was close up and personal, and ever so slightly contaminated by a smell, the like of which hadn't occurred since Paddy the Arab had farted in high-babies.

'Paul, I think I've been a bit of a prick,' Tom said, not alluding to me in any way at all, which came as something of a relief, and consequently I remained walking up the same side of the street with him.

'You have?' I enquired of my best friend and agent, who, it transpires, was also something of a prick.

'Yes, I have. We've been friends for years.' 'We have indeed, Tom,' I said. I was thirty-three, and I'd known Tom since I was five, which wasn't yesterday, or even the day before. Tom had once played football at the highest level, and I had looked on, but we had always been friends, doing the best we could do, which was pretty much all we could do.

'Anyway, the thing is, I don't think I've been much of a friend recently.' 'Oh?' I said, replying to the man who had been my best friend since forever.

'It's your drinking.' 'My drinking?' I said, referring to the

123

drinking that was no longer present, replaced as it was by soft drinks and sanity.

'Yeah. You see, I've known you've had a problem for years. And what did I do? I drank with you. Jesus Christ, even the other night in the restaurant, there I was drinking wine, never thinking for a second that it might have been a problem for you.' 'But Tom, trust me. I was grand in the restaurant. Honest.' 'You were fucked, Paul.' 'Well, I wouldn't say I was fucked, exactly . . . I was . . . ' 'Fucked?' 'Yeah, Tom. On reflection, fucked does not seem inaccurate, although it wasn't the wine that was causing me a problem, it was . . . I don't know, it's just difficult sometimes. I know I won't ever drink again. It's just that "ever again" seems . . . longer than I was expecting it to be.' 'I don't know what to say to you, Paul. I just want to apologise for being a . . . ' 'Prick? 'Yeah, a prick.' 'Tom, trust me. You're my best friend, and you are anything but a prick.

'OK, so you're a prick most of the time, but you're not a prick when it comes to me and my drinking, or not drinking. You once told me that I was a grown-up, and you know something? You were right. So please lay off this prick stuff, even if you are a bit of a prick. Tom, I drank because I drank, and you have no reason to apologise. Now drop it, OK?' 'OK.' 'Shite.' 'What?' 'I've just realised that you apologised to me.' 'So?' 'Tom, you never apologised to me for anything, ever. Any chance of getting that apology in writing?' 'No. Now seeing as how you've brought up the subject of writing, how is the new book coming along?' 'Fine.' 'You haven't written a single page, have you?' 'I have.' 'Honest?' 'Yeah.' 'May I ask how many pages?' 'No.' 'How many pages have you written, Paul?' 'Oh . . . ' 'How many pages, Paul?' 'Oh . . . you know . . . it's a first draft . . . I'd say . . . oh, I'd say . . . one.' 'Sorry, I didn't hear you correctly. I could have sworn you said . . . one.' 'Well, one is better than none, Tom.' 'One? You've written *one* page?' 'More or less.'

'More or less?' 'Well . . . it's not a full page . . . yet.' Tom then looked up towards the night sky and murmured something that sounded like 'Shite', although I could be wrong, but somehow I doubt it.

As the bottom of Grafton Street became the middle of Grafton Street became the top of Grafton Street, I found myself reflecting on my inability to write. Once I drank, and now I didn't. Once I could write, and now there is nothing. If I was honest with Tom, I would have told him why I couldn't come up with anything that would follow the house which had been sitting idle for several months past. I could have told Tom many things, but he would not have understood. I could have told him about the wallflower that had existed once upon a time in the past. I could have told him about how I would force that wallflower into retreat, if only for a time, thanks to something other than soft drinks.

And I could have told him about how, during the recent days which had become weeks, which had become months, the wallflower had returned, because I was now sane, and how I was now unable to write, because of that sanity. I could have told Tom many things, but he would not have understood.

I had walked up Grafton Street with a man who had been my best friend since forever, and I had told him many things, and left many things unsaid. One of the things I did tell him was that no apology was called for. Perhaps, at some point in the future, I will come to realise that I was wrong, and that an apology was most certainly called for. But that is in the future, and one can only speculate on words that have yet to be spoken by me.

And so it was that, in the present, I walked with my friend up Grafton Street, and two women walked in front of us, no doubt discussing the weather, and whatever else it is that women discuss whenever they walk up Grafton Street.

31

I am an octopus. I have been an octopus for some time now and I wish I was dead.

How it came to pass that I found myself transformed into an octopus is quite beyond me, but I can only state the facts as they are, and it started once upon a time, when I'd just finished eating a Big Mac and medium fries.

Having reached the top of Grafton Street, Claire and Suzanne turned onto St Stephen's Green, and myself and Tom did likewise. The two women continued to talk about this, that and whatever it is that women talk about whenever they turn onto St Stephen's Green, but the two men who were walking behind them said little, content to leave the other to his own thoughts as they reflected upon such matters as the meaning of life and page ones that had yet to become page twos.

Fifty or so yards after turning onto St Stephen's Green, Claire and Suzanne decided to walk down Dawson Street, and my legs were beginning to hurt.

Our voyage of discovery ended with a return visit to Grafton Street, and it was there that I suggested to Tom that a visit to McDonald's might be in order.

My travelling companion, who for some time now had been paying little or no attention to anything that was going on around him – lost as he was in a world of his own, a place that probably contained many things, including page ones that were nearing completion – asked me why I thought a visit to McDonald's might be in order, and I told him that Claire and Suzanne had just walked into McDonald's ahead of us, and I didn't have to say anything else, because Tom could see that I was talking sense, which was quite unusual, all things considered.

The four of us found a little candlelit table in the corner – which, give or take the candle, is not an entirely inaccurate description of it – and taking on a role previously performed by a waiter called Des O'Connor, whose absence could only be put down to the fact that he was probably making a dog's bollix of things elsewhere, I asked Claire, Suzanne and Tom what they would like to eat, and they told me, and I then asked them what they would like to drink, and they told me that too.

I then proceeded to make my way towards a counter of many smiling faces. One of the smiling faces said 'Hi', and I said 'Hello', and the smiling face then asked me what I would like, and I said that the cancellation of Third World debt seemed as good a place as any to start, although I didn't say that exactly, because I knew that the young smiling face was just doing his job, counting down the hours to the time when he could lose the face that was smiling and replace it with a face that would still be smiling, because that's what youthful faces do. I had little doubt, however, that the smile which was to come would be a smile which bore little resemblance to the smile that was currently in front of me: a facial expression that one would normally expect to encounter whenever paths cross with a born-again whatever-you're-having-yourself.

But because I was a writer who knew about life, I had the good sense to realise that the kid who was serving me was just doing his job. But because I knew about life, I also knew that if the kid's smile was a natural smile, this was someone who should never, ever be issued with a gun licence.

And so, having decided to cancel the cancellation of Third World debt, I proceeded to order four something-or-others from the nice young man who was smiling. All of the four something-or-others had the word 'meal' in their title, and I envied the person who had come up with such a description, because it was quite apparent to me that for the person concerned, writer's block had never entered into the equation.

With each meal there came a drink of your choice, and Claire chose coffee as her drink of choice, as did Suzanne, Tom and I. There were other drinks we could have chosen, each one of them soft and fizzy, except for the tea, which isn't soft or fizzy, because tea is just what it is, which is tea, but my dining companions and I had decided to go with the coffee because it seemed like a good idea at the time. There was no wine on the menu, which was a pity, because I'm reasonably certain that I would have handled myself somewhat better then the time previously, when insanity had run amok.

Returning to the small candlelit table that was missing a candle, and taking on a role previously performed by the artist called Des O'Connor, I handed each of my dining companions their meals and the accompanying drinks, although they had been under the impression that the drinks they had ordered were coffees, which they weren't, and I'm not really sure what they were.

Meals served, duty performed, I handed my dicky bow back to Des O'Connor before taking my place at the table beside Claire, who was seated beside Suzanne, who was seated beside Tom, who was seated beside me, because the small table we were seated at was round. Tom took a sip of his coffee, and then had a religious moment, making the briefest of references to Christ, which seemed slightly unusual for Tom, but there you have it.

The four of us sat side by side in a restaurant, or so the story goes, and we ate our meals, because it seemed like a pretty reasonable thing to do, although I'm not really sure if one should always do what one is expected to do.

We then found ourselves engaging in small talk, and it suited me, because the evening was coming to an end, and all in all I thought I had handled myself pretty well. The wallflower who was becoming ever-present had obviously decided to take the night off.

Tom talked about this, that and a book which would supposedly begin with the words 'There is a house', and how that book was short, bordering as it did on non-existent. I said nothing in response to this, because I now knew that the book would never be written.

Suzanne talked about this, that and a book which had yet to be written, and she made reference to the person who would be the author of that book by describing him as a writer who would deliver, because he always did. I said nothing in response to this, because I did not recognise the person that Suzanne was talking about.

Claire talked about this, that and the evening that had just passed, and she thanked me for inviting her to the book launch.

I then talked about this, that and the evening that had just passed, and I thanked Claire for thanking me, and I didn't say anything else, probably because I was getting embarrassed.

Conversation over, meals eaten – or something approximating to same – I was silently congratulating myself on the avoidance of dog's bollixes and other such trivia, when Claire said something which terrified me.

On the face of it, what Claire said seemed innocent enough, but the wallflower who was by now beginning to make his presence felt knew better, because he always did.

'Does anyone fancy going on to a club?' was the question posed: nothing too complicated.

Claire had asked the three of us if we fancied going on to a club, and although she was addressing everyone who was at the table with her, she was mostly looking at me and the wallflower who was now seated beside me, although Claire wouldn't have seen the wallflower who was now seated beside me because he mostly kept himself in the shadows, waiting for his moment to shine.

'Sounds great!' was Suzanne's reply to Claire.

'Club? Yeah, why not? Paul, what about you?' was Tom's response to Claire, a reply which also contained a question. Yes, Tom did indeed fancy going on to a club, but he also no longer wanted to be a prick. McDonald's is one thing, but my best friend would have known that nightclubs were quite different, containing as they do something other than soft drinks.

I looked at Tom and smiled. I'll be grand, my smile told him. Honest, yeah, I'll be grand.

'A club? Sounds great.' I had just informed Claire that her suggestion about us all going on to a nightclub sounded great. In truth, it sounded slightly less than great, but there was little else I could say.

But I also had another reason for telling Claire why her suggestion about walking through the gates of hell had sounded great, and I'd hoped he'd heard it. Because my reply to Claire, which on the face of it seemed pretty innocuous, was something other. It was a reply that had a secret message encoded within it: a something that only a wallflower could decipher. 'Fuck off' was the message to the wallflower, and I was soon to discover that the wallflower had indeed received my message, because he replied with a message of his own. 'Fuck off' was his message to me, and he then followed that up by making reference to a gobshite of his acquaintance.

And that was that. Accompanying Claire, Suzanne and Tom, I left McDonald's and headed off to a nightclub. And it was there that I became an octopus, courtesy of the wallflower who walked with me, and everything worked out just grand.

32

I am an octopus. I have been an octopus for some time now and I wish I were dead.

Once, a long time ago, I had looked on, glass of Coke in hand. In the nightclub of yesterday I could do little more than look on at the youths who had played football at the highest level, because dancing was not an option. I got rhythm, I got music, who could ask for anything more? I had no rhythm and I had no music – just a poxy glass of Coke. And as for the anything else? I didn't ask for it, but it just seemed like the right thing to do, and so, putting down the glass of Coke which had been with me since forever, I replaced it with something stronger, and I ended up getting both rhythm and music, and everything worked out just grand.

Once, at some point in the future, Kate Kowolski will tell me that her husband can't dance to save his life, but it doesn't matter, she'll tell me, because she didn't marry me for my dancing. Why she will have married me is difficult to say, but at some point in the future she will tell me that she loves me, and I guess that's as good a reason as any.

But fragmented conversations concerning the future have yet to occur, and in the present I sit in a nightclub, remembering a nightclub of my youth, when I said farewell to a wallflower and became the male equivalent of a dancing queen.

And in the place they call the present, I have yet to become an octopus, because I have yet to dance, and I will not dance, because I am incapable of dance, or anything else for that matter. I simply do what I do, which is nothing much, and nothing much is mostly what I now find myself doing. Sanity has enabled me to be myself, and I'm not a pretty sight.

Inches away from the dance floor, there is a candlelit table, and it is there that I sit.

The candle that is the centrepiece of the table isn't really a candle, because it's an electric light shaped like a candle, although that's got very little to do with anything, but it's important to get the details right. To the left of me sits Claire, and to the left of Claire sits Suzanne. Tom is seated to the left of Suzanne, and I am seated to the left of Tom, because the table we sit at is round. Apart from containing a candle that isn't really a candle, because it's really a light, the table also contains four drinks, one of which is soft and fizzy, and I know that I won't dance because I can't fucking well dance.

In fairness to him, I can't say that the wallflower didn't warn me.

'Gobshite,' he said, addressing me by name as we walked down Grafton Street, heading towards a place of no importance that just happened to be a nightclub, although I reasoned that by telling myself that a nightclub was a place of no importance I was behaving in a manner that seemed, on the face of it, pretty sane, because I didn't really fancy dwelling on the prospect of entering a nightclub that was getting closer with each step taken.

'You honestly think you can pull this off?' the wallflower asked me, and I didn't respond to the wallflower, because the answer was all too obvious.

'It's not too late, you know,' the wallflower informed me as we entered the nightclub.

But I ignored the wallflower, knowing that he spoke the truth; I also knew that I was a grown-up, and consequently, wallflowers shouldn't really exist when you're no longer a child, and totally sane.

Having said everything that had to be said, the wallflower retreated into the shadows, in anticipation of the octopus to come, and I wanted to drink something other than a soft drink, but I didn't, because I was now all grown up.

Upon our arrival at the table, Tom ordered drinks from a woman who looked nothing like Des O'Connor and I started to engage my companions in conversations that covered everything and anything under the sun. I knew that by engaging my companions in conversations that covered everything and anything under the sun, the possibility that I might find myself dancing would recede with each passing moment, and so on the face of it everything seemed to make sense.

The woman who looked nothing like Des O'Connor arrived with our drinks, and everything was starting to go according to plan – if you can call insanity a plan. The four of us talked about such diverse subjects as intensive care, and how serious it was, and the weather, and how interesting it was. We even discussed politics, when Suzanne made some comment about George Bush; this led to Tom referring to the president of the United States as a dangerous, psychotic lunatic – which seemed a bit unreasonable, but there you have it.

We talked and we talked and we talked, and our talking had lasted for five minutes and fifteen seconds. Five minutes and sixteen seconds after our talking began, Suzanne asked Tom if he would like to dance, and Tom informed her that yes, he would indeed like to dance.

As is the way with these things, Tom and Suzanne took to the floor together, and I found myself asking Claire if intensive care was an interesting place to work, and she said that it was, and I didn't ask her to dance because I bloody well couldn't.

Elsewhere, in another dimension, Mick Jagger was complaining about a lack of satisfaction, and Suzanne and Tom danced with him. Someone other than me in my situation would have asked Claire if she wanted to dance, and I wanted to be that someone, but I wasn't, and because I was just me I couldn't ask Claire if she wanted to dance. I felt like an adolescent who didn't know his arse from his elbow.

Thanks to the freeing up of one of her hands, Suzanne was able to wave over at us from the dance floor. Prior to this, the hand that waved at us had been keeping company with her other hand, both of them positioned several inches above her head as they flapped this way and that, and God knows where else, and whose movements had been designed to express some sort of sympathy for Mick Jagger and his satisfaction, or lack of it. And now, although one of Suzanne's hands remained airborne, the hand that was not flapping was clearly encouraging me and Claire to join Suzanne and Tom on the dance floor.

But if I obeyed the command of the hand that was not flapping, I would inevitably end up doing what one would normally do, which was to dance. But I passed on the offer of a dance from the hand that was not flapping, because I couldn't dance, because I was drinking something that was soft and fizzy. Instead, I just smiled back at the hand that was not flapping, although I can't be entirely certain as to the status of that smile, because the expression on my face probably suggested a bad case of piles.

Looking away from Suzanne, I looked at Claire, who was looking at me, and I could see by the expression on her face that she was about to ask me a question, and I wanted to go home because I knew that Claire was about to ask me to dance. But Claire didn't ask me to dance. Instead, she asked me to tell her about my daughter, and I told Claire that my daughter was now twelve, and that she was beautiful, and that I loved her. Claire then asked me about how often I saw Jessica, and I said not often. I then told Claire the truth, by informing her about my decision not to see my daughter for a while, because I wanted to . . . I'm not really sure what I said exactly, but I think I might have made the briefest of references to the weeks which had sometimes contained days which were less than seven in number, and how I wanted to be sure that the weeks of the future would all begin on Monday and end on Sunday, although I didn't say that exactly, preferring instead to couch my past in the vaguest of terms by referring to myself as someone who used to drink too much, but who was now grand, and I left out the part about me being totally fucked, because I thought it was for the best. Claire then said something about it being none of her business, but even though it was none of her business, she went on to tell me that she thought it was really sad that I hadn't seen my young daughter in the last couple of years, and she finished by apologising, because she knew it was none of her business, and I told Claire that no apology was necessary because what she had said was true.

Claire then smiled at me and told me that she was sure everything would work out, and I smiled back at Claire, probably because she was really nice.

I had talked to Claire, and Claire had talked to me, and I had totally forgotten about the dance floor which was inches away from our table, and I think that had something to do with Claire.

Suzanne and her dancing partner returned to our table, and I noticed that Mick Jagger had been forced to give way to Simply Red, who were in the process of holding back the years.

I knew that I wanted to dance, and I knew that I couldn't, so I asked Claire if she would like to dance, because I figured that even I could shuffle about a dance floor, slow-dancing with a woman who was very nice, and Claire informed me that she would like to dance very much.

As we left the table, Suzanne and Tom smiled at me, and I smiled back at them because I just did, even if I was terrified. Simply Red I could do; anything else was a recipe for disaster. No, get up and dance, I told myself, and when the song is over, leave the dance floor before things are moved up a gear or two.

So Claire and I took to the floor, and in the shadows a somewhat subdued wallflower looked on.

And so it is that once upon a time in the future, legend will have it that I danced with a woman called Claire, and that a woman called Claire danced with me.

I held Claire around the waist and she put her hands on my shoulders, which probably made sense. I moved my feet this way and that, that way and this, and Claire's hair smelt lovely.

Holding back the years – it wasn't that difficult and I was in severe danger of actually enjoying myself.

The music played and everything was grand. Soon the song would be over and I would thank Claire for dancing with me and, dancing completed, sanity restored, I would return to the table, accompanied by the woman who was very nice.

It was Joan O'Neill's fortieth birthday. This might seem to have nothing to do with anything, and for the most part, it doesn't. But it's the part that *does* that proved problematic.

The reason I knew it was Joan O'Neill's fortieth

birthday was because the DJ had abruptly stopped Simply Red holding back the years as he proceeded to tell everyone and anyone that it was Joan O'Neill's fortieth birthday, and consequently everyone and anyone, me excluded, proceeded to clap and cheer Joan O'Neill as she was dragged onto the dance floor by friends and family. The DJ then informed everyone and anyone, me included, that Joan O'Neill's favourite song was called 'Take On Me' and 'Take On Me' was sung by A-Ha, and I knew enough about classical music to know that A-Ha would be wanting someone to take them on at a speed that was not slow, and I also knew that the slow dance with which I had been involved was now gone, replaced as it was by madness, and I was terrified.

What to do? I asked myself. Shite, I told myself.

I stood surrounded by people who had both rhythm and music. In truth, many of them had neither, but they didn't give a damn and it didn't really matter. Claire had both rhythm and music, a fact which was all too evident as she moved her body this way and that, that way and this, inches away from me.

I had two choices, neither of which was very attractive, and I was caught like a frightened bunny in the glare of a wallflower. I could leave the dance floor, or I could stay. Leaving would have required much explanation, and I was too sane to think straight. I had the good sense to realise that if I was to stay on the dance floor, I would have to do something which would be an improvement on the situation which currently prevailed: namely myself, and a total absence of movement. Because I was a grown-up, I decided to stay, and because I decided to stay, I decided to dance. Shite.

Moving my left leg in and my right leg out, I proceeded

to shake them all about, because it seemed like the right thing to do. I then smiled at Claire and she smiled at me, which was nice of her, all things considered. I had never in my life danced without the benefit of assistance from elsewhere, and because the glass I'd left behind me on the table contained nothing stronger than liquid that was soft and fizzy, I found myself entering totally uncharted waters, and I was screwed.

And elsewhere, dancing right beside me, a wallflower looked on, unable to contain his laughter.

I danced, my heart pounded and I was scared shitless.

I couldn't but help notice that Claire was moving both feet and arms, and so I decided to do likewise, because I figured that dancing was not restricted to legs alone. I'm not sure which arm I had decided to move first, and it doesn't really matter, but move it I did, and it was quickly followed by the movement of whichever arm had remained static by my side.

And so I was to find myself dancing the dance of the damned, and I wanted to run to God knows where, because I was only too well aware of the fact that my dancing was but a metaphor for my life.

Arms moving this way and that, and other places psychiatric, I became an octopus, dancing with the confidence of a child I had once known, and as he danced, the octopus knew that he must have appeared pretty pathetic to all who were watching him, and his audience was large.

Eventually the dance ended, and the man who accompanied Claire from the dance floor had once again become a traveller through time – a child who could do little more than look on – and he knew that for him, the future was pretty much all it had ever been.

As we left the dance floor, Claire put a hand around my waist, trying to support the unsupportable, and it was all she could do. She had seen for herself the real me, and because she was nice, she said nothing.

And somewhere else, in another place, a wallflower who had spoken the truth whispered my name, and that name was 'Gobshite'.

33

Gobshite.

If I should die before I wake, I pray to God that God will exist, because it would be pretty pointless praying to God otherwise. What happens to us when we die? Not sure.

Perhaps we just end up doing something that isn't too complicated. Makes sense. We might just sit there, wherever, discussing the weather.

'Grand day, thank God' – sinner.

'Yeah, grand day' – saint.

'Is that that, then?' – sinner.

'Yeah, guess so' – saint.

'See you same time tomorrow?' – sinner.

'Yeah, why not?' – saint.

'It might rain tomorrow' – sinner.

'You think?' – saint.

'No' – sinner.

'I can't remember the rain' – saint.

'Neither can I, but it was probably nice' – sinner.

'It never rains' – saint.

'No' – sinner.

'What time is it?' – saint.

'Not sure. It's probably the same time as yesterday' – sinner.

'What time was it yesterday?' – saint.

'Not sure. It was probably the same time as today' – sinner.

'See you same time tomorrow then?' – saint.

'Yeah, why not' – sinner.

'Excuse me?'

(Enter stage left, or stage right, depending on your point of view, a someone of no particular importance who has just asked to be excused, because it seemed like the right thing to do.)

'Yes?' – saint/sinner.

'I think I'm lost' – the someone of no particular importance.

'Lost?' – saint/sinner.

'Yes, lost' – the someone of no particular importance.

'You must be new' – saint.

'New?' – the someone of no particular importance.

'Not old' – sinner.

'No, I'm not new. I'm old, I think. Although I could be wrong' – the someone of no particular importance.

'He's new' – saint.

'Yeah, he's new' – sinner.

'Am I in Leitrim?' – the someone of no particular importance.

'What is Leitrim?' – saint/sinner.

'Leitrim is a something or other, somewhere or other, although I couldn't be entirely certain what or where' – the someone of no particular importance.

'Well, this isn't Leitrim. We'd know if it was Leitrim' – saint.

'Yeah, we'd know if it was Leitrim' – sinner.

'Would you mind if I sat down? I'm old and I need to rest' – the someone of no particular importance.

'You're not old. You're new. Sit, and it will all make sense' – saint.

'It will?' – the someone of no particular importance.

'Yes' – sinner.

'Sure looks like Leitrim' – the someone of no particular importance.

'What does Leitrim look like?' – saint/sinner.

'Leitrim looks like Cavan' – the someone of no particular importance.

'What is Cavan?' – saint/sinner.

'Cavan is a something or other, somewhere or other, although I couldn't be entirely certain what or where' – the someone of no particular importance.

'Well, this isn't Cavan. We'd know if it was Cavan' – sinner.

'Yeah, we'd know if it was Cavan' – saint.

'Grand day, thank God' – the someone of no particular importance.

'Yeah, grand day' – saint/sinner.

'See you same time tomorrow?' – the someone of no particular importance.

'See you same time yesterday?' – sinner.

'See you same time today?' – saint.

'It might rain tomorrow' – the someone of no particular importance.

'It might rain yesterday' – sinner.

'It might rain today' – saint.

'You think?' – the someone of no particular importance.

'No' – saint/sinner.

'Makes sense' – the someone of no particular importance.

'It could be Leitrim' – saint.

'It could be Cavan' – sinner.

'No, I'd know if it was Leitrim or Cavan' – the someone of no particular importance.

'Well, it's probably somewhere' – saint.

'Do you dance here?' – the someone of no particular importance.

'No, we don't dance' – saint/sinner.

'Are you sure you don't dance?' – the someone of no particular importance.

'Quite sure' – saint/sinner.

'I think I know where we are' – the someone of no particular importance.

'You do?' – saint/sinner.

'Yes, I do' – the someone of no particular importance.

'Where are we?' – saint/sinner.

'We are in heaven' – the someone of no particular importance.

'What is heaven?' – saint.

'This is heaven' – the someone of no particular importance.

'Is this not Leitrim?' – sinner.

'No, they dance in Leitrim. Leitrim is hell' – the someone of no particular importance.

'Is this not Cavan?' – saint.

'No, they dance in Cavan. Cavan is hell' – the someone of no particular importance.

'What is a dance?' – sinner.

'I'm not sure, but I did it once' – the someone of no particular importance.

'What did you do?' – saint/sinner.

'I danced with a girl once and everything was grand' – the someone of no particular importance.

'What does "grand" mean?' – saint/sinner.

'"Grand" is totally fucked up, and there's not really much more that can be said about grand' – the someone of no particular importance.

'So, you say this is heaven?' – saint.

'Yes, this is heaven' – the someone of no particular importance.

'It is not Leitrim?' – sinner.

'No, they dance in Leitrim' – the someone of no particular importance.

'It is not Cavan?' – saint.

'No, they dance in Cavan' – the someone of no particular importance.

'So that's that then?' – sinner.

'Guess so' – the someone of no particular importance.

'Grand day, thank God' – saint.

'Yeah, grand day' – the someone of no particular importance.

'It never rains' – sinner.

'No, it never rains' – the someone of no particular importance.

'Gobshite' – wallflower.

Gobshite. He *did* warn me. But would I listen? No. Dance, I told myself. Dance and be a man, I told myself. So I danced and I danced and I danced, and everything worked out just grand, because it just didn't. I sit at the candlelit table that supports the candle that isn't really a candle, and I am a man who isn't really a man, and I want to die and move on elsewhere – to Leitrim or Cavan or wherever.

Having completed the dance of the damned, I returned to the table with Claire, and I had the good sense to realise that even though I wasn't the greatest dancer in the world, I wasn't quite as bad as I perceived myself to be, because such a thing was impossible. However, within seconds of returning to my seat, I was to realise that there was no such thing as the impossible, and that the dreaming of the impossible dream, or nightmare, or whatever, was not just a dream: it was a horrible reality.

Tom asked me was I OK, and Suzanne asked me if I wanted to go home. Had my total and absolutely psychotic screw-up on the dance floor really been that obvious? Perhaps.

Perhaps not. Tom's query regarding my being OK could have been put down to the fact that in a previous conversation that had lasted for five minutes and fifteen seconds we'd already discussed everything that there was to discuss, and now the only thing that remained up for discussion was me, which would have been nice of him, if that was indeed the case. And Suzanne's query regarding my going home could simply have been a result of the fact that it was getting late and it was probably past my bedtime, which would have been nice of her, if that was indeed the case. But that was not the case, because the case in question could best be filed under head case, something that became all too obvious when the woman who had been my dancing partner took me by the hand and proceeded to inform me in a tone of voice that was both gentle and nice that she was tired, and that she wanted to get some fresh air before she went home. I knew that Claire just wanted rid of me, which was perfectly understandable, all things considered, until she asked me if I'd like to accompany her in her quest for fresh air – a remark that was *not* perfectly understandable, all things considered.

Myself and Claire said our goodbyes to Tom and Suzanne, and Claire proceeded to kiss Tom on the cheek, and followed that up by kissing Suzanne on the cheek. I then took centre stage by kissing Suzanne on the cheek, although I didn't kiss Tom anywhere, probably because he was my agent.

But Tom was to whisper a sweet nothing in my ear as I left his company: a sweet nothing to the effect that I should take care of myself, because . . . and he didn't say much else. He just looked at me and smiled, and I smiled back at the man who had been my best friend since forever. At some point in the future, Tom will tell me about how wrecked I looked as I left his company, but because the future is not in the present, one can only speculate on conversations yet to occur, and in the place they call the present Tom simply smiled at me, because it was pretty much all he could do.

And so I left the nightclub in the company of Claire, and because I was to find myself walking her home, it was a journey that took over two hours to complete. And as we walked, I told Claire almost everything that there was to tell about me.

And as I talked, a wallflower temporarily retreated into the darkness.

34

In my dreams there is a house. I sit on a river bank looking across at that house. The house is old, as is the river in front of me. Beneath waters that are crystal clear, fish make their way towards somewhere else, because that's just the way of things, I guess.

Occasionally a fish will momentarily break the surface of the still waters and nature's silence will be broken by the sound of a plop. No sooner will the plop have begun to recede than another plop will take its place, as the fish does what it has to do and returns to its rightful place beneath the surface.

I am old, and I am surrounded by my future. A child is playing in the grounds of the house, her beauty framed by the green swath of ivy which climbs its walls, foliage which serves as a reminder to all who might pass that the empty shell which stands before them is not of this time but of another: a mute witness bearing testament to that other time, the time when there was a living house beyond the now, beyond reality.

How it came to pass that the child is playing on the other side of the river is something of a mystery to me. Perhaps elsewhere, not too far away, there is a bridge, and if so, it is there that she would have crossed. Perhaps. Perhaps not. The only thing I can say with absolute certainty is that the child's journey would have begun once upon a time in the past, when her grandmother exchanged Valentine's cards with the old man who is now looking on: a simple act that was the beginning of a love affair between a man and a woman, and which would lead to the birth of a child who, or so the story goes, would one day give birth to a child of her own.

The old man looks on, being ever-careful to keep a watchful eye on the child in case she should fall. But if she fell, he would pick her up and hold her closely to him, and in so doing he would become a make-things-better man who would wipe away the tears of a granddaughter as he made good on a silent promise of long ago, when he had first set eyes on his infant daughter.

The mother of the child who is playing on the other side of the river is no longer an infant, but her father loves her, because I always did. Once, a long time ago, I went away for a while because I was sane, but that is in the past, and although it is of some relevance, it is the actions of today that matter most to the man who is now old.

And today, the old man still loves Jessica's mother, because I always did, and Caroline still loves me, because she always did. But life being what it is, it did what it usually does, which is usually the best that it can do, and although they are still very much part of each other's lives, the man and the woman who exchanged Valentine's cards once upon a time in the distant past have chosen to travel different paths, but that's OK, I guess, because some things were always meant to be.

I am old, and I am surrounded by my future. I sit on a river bank. Beside me there is a picnic basket that contains apples, oranges, sandwiches, lemonade and a flask of coffee.

The woman who is sitting beside me made the coffee, because she has been telling me for several years that I couldn't make a cup of coffee to save my life.

Kate Conroy used to be Kate Kowolski, but once, a long time ago, I asked her to marry me and she said yes, and so Kate Kowolski became Kate Conroy and everything worked out just grand, because it just did.

Kate Conroy sits beside me on a river bank, and she is wearing a dress that is coloured red and blue and green and white, although some would say that the white is more creamy than white, but I'm an old man, and she looks gorgeous. Myself and Kate Conroy are now both older than we once were, but she still wears mad pyjamas, and I love her and she loves me.

And elsewhere, sitting right beside me, there is a wall-flower who has been ever-present since forever. Once, a long time ago, I came to the realisation that the wallflower was just a part of me, nothing more and nothing less, and so I asked the wallflower if he wanted to come along for the ride, and he said 'Grand', and I said 'Fine.'

I am old, and I am surrounded by my future. I know nothing about the house that sits across the river, save for the fact that it is part of my destiny. Its location is a complete mystery to me, but I know it exists. It has to exist. If it doesn't, I'm toast, and I don't want to be toast as I sit on a river bank with the woman who used to be my neighbour and who shares my love for the child who is playing in the grounds of a house, silently exploring this and that.

Once upon a time in the future, I will partake of a scene that contains both beauty and peace, and the only sound I will hear will be the occasional plop that comes from an adjacent river, and everything will be grand.

35

I walked with Claire down Westmoreland Street. It was late and my friend with the umbrella was nowhere to be seen. Eyes now shut, he was probably elsewhere, dreaming simple dreams concerning the magnificence of things to come. In a few hours' time the sun would rise and my friend with the umbrella would walk out into the daylight doing what came most naturally to him, totally unaware of the fact that he was mad. I knew that my friend was mad because sane people do not smile at complete strangers on Westmoreland Street, carrying little more than an umbrella. From time to time, and for reasons best known to themselves, a complete stranger would return the compliment and smile at the man who had just smiled at them, but that probably just meant that they were also mad. I, too, would occasionally come across my friend with the umbrella, and even though he would inevitably smile at me and I would inevitably smile at him, that probably had nothing to do with anything, because he was mad and I was now sane, and besides, he was my friend.

Leaving the street of a thousand smiles behind us, Claire and I continued on our journey, eventually arriving at Dorset Street, and it was there that we stopped at a chipper and shared a bag of chips.

Prior to the sharing of chips, we had made our way up O'Connell Street, surrounded by places that sold many things, including stamps and burgers and knickers that my mother probably never wore, but even if she did, I didn't want to know about it, and it was on O'Connell Street that I was to find myself telling Claire that I thought I was going insane, which probably seemed a bit strange, all things considered, but there you have it.

Claire then asked me why I thought I was going insane, and I told her about someone who had never belonged, a period in time bookended by the watching of football matches from afar and the recent dancing of a dance performed by a gobshite. Claire responded to me by saying that, while she didn't feel qualified to comment on the watching of football matches that had taken place long ago, the one event she did feel qualified to comment on was the event of the recent past, and she told me that even though I was almost certainly the worst dancer she had ever seen in her life, that didn't necessarily make me a gobshite because, she said, John Travolta had never won a Nobel Prize for anything, and I was to find myself wondering just what in hell did John Travolta have to do with anything, which I thought was quite reasonable on my part, all things considered.

As we made our way past the Gate Theatre, I was to find myself telling Claire about how sick I was of moaning to everyone and anyone about everything and anything, and when Claire asked me what I meant by this, I told her about how, in recent months, I had moaned on and on to almost anyone who would listen about the poor little-boy-lost that was me, and I cited herself, Caroline and my neighbour, Kate Kowolski as prime examples of people who were in receipt of my moans, and I told Claire that the time had now come for me to stop my moaning and start behaving in a manner befitting a grown adult.

Claire then asked me how I thought grown adults

behaved, and I told her I wasn't sure but I was reasonably certain they didn't behave like me.

We shared a bag of chips, and as we walked down Dorset Street Claire linked my arm and said something about it being a grand evening, and I agreed with her, because it was indeed a grand evening, even if it was now the early hours of the morning.

Claire then said something to me about my writing, by making reference to the page one which had yet to become page two, and when I told her that I had nothing to write about, Claire asked me if I was dead, and when I said no, Claire said that I had plenty to write about, which made some sort of sense, I suppose.

Two hours after leaving the nightclub, we arrived at Claire's front door, and Claire asked me if I wanted to come in for a coffee. I thanked her but said that I couldn't, because I had to get up early the next morning so that I could start writing again.

Claire smiled at me when I said that, and I was once again to find myself apologising to her for moaning about this, that and everything known to man. Claire told me that no apology was necessary because, she said, we were friends, and that's what friends were for.

Claire had mentioned the 'F' word, and I was glad that Claire had mentioned the 'F' word, because I wanted so much to be friends with Claire, and the reason I wanted so much to be friends with Claire was because friends don't go to bed with each other, even if the thought had crossed my mind as we walked arm in arm up Dorset Street sharing a bag of chips. But I was also pretty certain that the level of my sanity was such that my performance in the bedroom would not have been dissimilar to my performance on the dance floor, and I suddenly got a mental image of John Travolta with a poker stuck up his arse, which might seem a bit extreme but there you have it.

I liked Claire a lot. She was nice. She was considerate. She was caring. She was also very attractive. And she was my friend. If Claire had given any thought to the idea of herself and John Travolta going to bed together, she didn't say and I didn't ask. Perhaps it's a man thing: man meets woman, man and woman share a bag of chips, man sleeps with woman, woman discovers that John Travolta isn't everything he's cracked up to be, by virtue of the fact that he's cracked. Perhaps. Perhaps not. Some would say that women are from Venus, men are from Mars, but I'm probably from some place elsewhere, once captured in a picture I composed in high-babies, when Miss O'Mahony had asked me to paint whatever I thought would come next.

Because Claire was my friend, I thought it best to give my friend a goodnight kiss on the cheek, and so I did. Because I was Claire's friend, she was obviously thinking the same thing as me, which is why she kissed me on my cheek.

We then stood facing each other in silence for a second or two, and I can only blame Claire for this, because I was sane and I didn't know what to say. Eventually Claire cracked, and broke the silence. She also smiled. It was the smile of a friend. It was a nice smile. It was a pleasant smile. It was also an absolutely fucking gorgeous smile, and if it wasn't for the fact that I was John Travolta, I'm not sure if I could have restrained myself, but I did, because I just did.

'So, you?' Silence. John Travolta has left the building.

'Paul? 'Yeah?' 'Paul?' 'Yes?' 'Are you still with us?' 'Sorry, Claire, I was just . . . thinking.' 'Thinking?' 'Yes, Claire. I was just thinking about . . . things.' 'You were thinking about . . . things?' 'Erm . . . yes.' 'What things, Paul?' 'Erm . . . you . . . things.' 'You were thinking about me . . . things?' 'Erm . . . yes.'

'And what are these things you were thinking about?' 'Oh . . . oh . . . oh, just that you're . . . nice and . . . gorgeous . . . and . . . things.' 'Nice *and* gorgeous?' 'Erm . . . yeah . . . Sorry I didn't . . . ' I didn't get the chance to get beyond 'I didn't', and the reason I didn't get the chance to get beyond 'I didn't' was because Claire kissed me, and as the aforementioned kiss was on the lips and not on the cheek, my inability to get beyond 'I didn't' isn't really that surprising, all things considered, and there were quite a lot of things to consider.

The kiss lasted forever, and I returned Claire's kiss with a kiss of my own, because it seemed like the right thing to do, and besides, my lips were more or less adjacent to the lips of Claire Casey, so on the face of it, everything seemed to make sense.

Eventually, the kiss ended with Claire whispering something into my ear, and that something was this: 'Paul Conroy, I want you to listen to me. You are a writer, and that is something quite special. I want you to promise me that you will write many books. Good books, bad books, I don't care. Just write those books, because they will be yours. I want you to promise me that you will start to enjoy life. You have a daughter. Share your life with that daughter. Don't wait until your life changes for the better. Perhaps things will only start to get better when you become reacquainted with your daughter. Paul Conroy, you are without doubt the worst dancer I have ever come across in my life. But you know what? Big deal. Some people can dance, some people can't dance. It's not the end of the world. At least you are blessed with the knowledge that you can't dance, and if you should ever doubt that, I'd be glad to provide references. Paul, you told me that you moan a lot. Maybe you do, maybe you don't. I can only say that during the short time that I've known you, you moaned very little. Well, actually you moaned quite a lot. Hell, you even moaned about moaning, but that's OK. You see, the thing is, you've got a life. A good life? A bad life? Who's to say? There's only one person who can say that, Paul, and that person is you. Trust me when I say that you are one of the nicest blokes I have ever met, and that these past few days have been quite special for me. Paul, I suspect that you might have a long way to travel before you get to wherever it is that you're going, but I have little doubt that you'll get there, because the person I saw on the dance floor tonight wasn't some idiot. No, the person I saw was someone who was terrified, but someone who stood up to that terror and took to that dance floor. At some point in the future, Paul, you are going to share your life with someone very special. I do not know who that someone will be, but whoever they are, they will have a wonderful life, and the reason they will have a wonderful life is because they will be sharing it with you. But that time isn't now, because you have things to do, Paul Conroy. You have a daughter to meet, and you have books to write. So do me a favour. Go out into the world, young man, and embrace it, because the world needs people like you, although you might want to avoid embracing the odd dance floor.' Having finished whispering her Dear John letter into my ear, Claire Casey kissed me on the cheek. She also smiled at me, and her smile told me that everything would be OK.

Her Dear John letter hadn't been a kiss-off, although it *was* a goodbye. No, Claire Casey had merely whispered some home truths in my ear, and I was grateful to her for that.

I think, although I couldn't be sure, that we shook hands, although it probably wasn't a handshake as such. It was more a case of one hand gently brushing against another, as two friends said a final farewell.

As she closed her front door, Claire smiled at me one final time, and that was that.

Somewhere on Dorset Street, close to a chipper I once knew, I hailed a taxi. The taxi stopped, but I told the driver to ignore my raised hand. It was a grand evening, and because of this I had decided to walk home, so that I could think about the many things that now needed doing.

I would see Jessica, I would write a book, and everything was now possible.

I knew this because I once had a friend who told me it was so.

36

Things to do and people to see.

When I awoke the following morning, I knew that I was at last free to do many things, and so I jumped out of bed enthused with life, before lying back down again, because I wasn't as young as I used to be.

Things to do and people to see.

Today I will write many words: big words, small words, in-between words. I will write the words that need writing, because I am a writer and that's what writers do. And having finished the sculpturing of something out of nothing, I will ring the house I used to call home, and if Jessica should answer the phone, all the better, because I'm her father and I love her, and I will tell Jessica that I love her, because that's what fathers do.

If Caroline should answer the phone, that's OK too, because I will tell Caroline that I am now a picture of health, and Caroline will be pleased to hear that all is well in the world of me.

Things to do and people to see.

Having decided on my itinerary for the day, I slowly climbed out of bed and put on my dressing gown. In the corner of my living room there is a word processor, and, leaving my bedroom, it was there that I headed. On the word processor there is a switch, and for the first time in many days, I flicked on that switch. The word processor did not respond to the flicking on of the switch, and so I plugged in the plug that was situated on the wall beside the word processor and everything worked out grand, because I wasn't a rocket scientist.

I was now a writer who had decided to write, and so I decided to make myself a cup of coffee. Opening the fridge, I came upon a carton of milk which had a 'best before' date stamped on it, and as that date was yesterday's date, I decided that I could write.

My pack of twenty cigarettes had twelve cigarettes in it and, doing the maths, I calculated that I would be able to write for three hours before having to go to the shops, and I knew that I could write quite a lot in three hours.

I am a writer, and I have decided to write. In front of me there is a screen. On that screen there are some words, and I will build on those words, because that is what writers do.

There is a house . . .

No problem. It will come. Yeah, it will come; it always did, or so the story goes.

I have now been writing for fifteen minutes, and my twenty pack of twelve has become a twenty pack of ten. The mug of coffee that sits in front of me contains a spoon full of coffee, two sugars, and seagull droppings that have a 'best before' date on them of yesterday. I have decided to stick with the cigarettes and forego the coffee, because I'm a writer, and I know about these things.

There is a house . . .

Perhaps I should ask Caroline out to lunch? Makes sense. Might be better than just ringing the house. Yeah, she'd like that. Just like old times. But in the old times Caroline didn't have to support me, so it might be better if I didn't ask Caroline to lunch until I'm in a position to repay her every last cent that she's lent me. But if I was to wait until I'd repaid Caroline every last cent that she's lent me, Caroline and I would probably be waiting quite a long time to have that lunch, because Caroline has lent me quite a few cents.

Things to do and people to see.

Start writing.

I *am* writing.

What are you writing?

Stuff.

What stuff?

This stuff.

This stuff?

There-is-a-house stuff.

How's it going?

Grand.

I could always just ring her and say that I'd like to drop up to the house.

You could.

Yeah, and I could tell her that I've decided to get down to some serious writing, and that I'll be in a position to pay back every last cent that she's lent me, just as soon as the royalties start to flow in.

You could.

What do you think?

I think it makes perfect sense.

You do?

I do.

That's that, then?

Yep.

Things to do and people to see.

There is a house . . .

Where are you, House? What secrets do you hold? Once, a long time ago, you were the setting for something. But what was that something? Was that something sad? Tragic?

Happy? A love affair gone wrong? A love affair gone right? If it is a love affair, who's in love with whom? Perhaps, House, you have nothing to do with the main storyline. If you're a prologue, that would make some kind of sense. He loves her, and she loves him. But who is he? Perhaps he's just passing through, on his way to somewhere else. What is his name?

You could always call him Paul.

No, Paul would be too self-indulgent, and besides, he'd be shite in bed.

Gerald?

No, he's a gobshite, and besides, he knows about wall-flowers and stuff, and that makes me nervous.

Jack?

Jack sounds good.

But who is Jack and where is he going?

He's going away. He's going home.

But where is home?

America?

Sounds good.

But why is he going home?

He's going home because he's travelled around Europe and seen most all that there is to see.

So he's wealthy?

No, he's poor, I think.

But how is he getting home?

Not sure. I think I'll send him home on a boat.

A boat?

Yeah. The story will probably be set in the early part of the twentieth century, so Ryanair won't have been invented yet.

So if he's poor, how will he be able to afford the price of his ticket?

Not sure. I think he might win it in a raffle or something.

A raffle?

Yeah, a raffle.

Do you not think that a raffle sounds too far-fetched?

You're probably right. Might have to rethink the raffle.

I have an idea.

You have?

Yes. Does he play cards?

Not sure. Why?

He could always win his ticket in a card game.

You think?

I do.

It might work.

I think it could.

You might be right.

OK, so we have a bloke called Jack who wins a boat ticket in a card game?

Yeah.

What then?

He meets Monica.

Who is Monica?

Monica is the woman he'll fall in love with.

Monica?

Yes.

Are we sure we want to run with Monica?

What's wrong with Monica?

Monica sounds too much like . . . Monica.

You don't think she should be called Monica?

No, I think Rose might be better.

Rose?

Yeah, Rose certainly works for me.

Rose? I must admit that the name has potential.

Well, it sure as hell beats Monica.

Is Rose poor?

No, Rose is wealthy, I think.

And Rose is on the boat?

Yeah.

And Jack and Rose fall in love?

Yeah.

And what happens then?

Not sure, although I think that Jack might end up dying near the end.

What happens? Does he drown?

No, he'll end up marrying Rose, and he'll die of a broken heart when Rose runs off with Timothy.

Who is Timothy?

Timothy is a French acrobat Rose was introduced to on board, but before they have the chance to get to know one another, the boat hits something or other, possibly Greenland, and the boat sinks, and Rose assumes that Timothy drowned, only he didn't, because an alien spacecraft saved him just as he was about to go under, and having taken him off to their home world, he is forced to perform his acrobatics for ten seasons on the alien equivalent of *The Late Late Show*, until he is eventually replaced by Ulick O'Connor, who takes up where Timothy left off, and who then proceeds to break Timothy's record by performing non-stop for twenty seasons. Anyway, content with Ulick, the aliens bring Timothy back to Earth, and upon his return he will meet Rose at a circus one night, and Rose will then realise that it was Timothy she loved all along, and the two of them will run off together and join a circus elsewhere, and Jack will die of his broken heart.

One small criticism?

Certainly.

That is such shite.

The story?

No, the name: Timothy. For God's sake, you can't call him Timothy.

Malcolm?

Malcolm could work.

That's that then.

Yeah, you seem to have it stitched.

Call it a day?

Yeah, why not.

Grand.

One question.

Yes?

Just where does the house come in?

Not sure.

Fair enough.

Shite.

What?

I just drank some of the coffee.

Are we finished?

Yeah.

There's always tomorrow.

You think?

Yeah.

Shite.

Yeah.

Build it and they will come. Still, it was all right for Kevin Costner. All he had to do was build a bloody baseball field. Building a novel is quite a different matter. Not to worry; there's always tomorrow or, failing that, the day after. The important thing is that I've made a start about making a start, and who knows what tomorrow, or the day after, might bring.

Shite.

37

Once upon a time, following on from the sharing of a bag of chips, Claire Casey had whispered into my ear words which encouraged me to start life anew. The journey from old world to new was never going to be an easy one, and many obstacles would lie in my path, the most obvious of them being me. But me or no me, it was a journey that had to be made, and so I began my journey by writing again, and what I wrote was nothing.

But having gone to the trouble of picking myself up and dusting myself down, I reasoned that my current tendency towards the writing of nothing was little more than a temporary aberration, and even if that was not the case, I knew that it was better to dwell amongst self-delusions concerning things temporary than to face up to realities which hinted at a writer's block that was now ever-present.

Doing the only thing that could be done, I sat at my kitchen table drinking a cup of coffee and smoking a cigarette. Several minutes earlier, I had gone to the shop and bought myself a carton of milk and a pack of twenty cigarettes to accompany the pack of twenty that had become a pack of five, and consequently I was now free to smoke away to my heart's content, and if my heart wasn't content, I was sure it would let me know, because hearts that are broken usually have a way of making themselves heard.

Freed at last from the clichéd shackles of my past, I knew

that there were many things that needed doing, and although I wasn't entirely certain what this Pandora's box of many other things that needed doing contained, contain them it did, and do them I would, because a friend had told me it was so.

Things to do and people to see.

11.30 AM. Writing over, job well done – or something approximating to same – I sat at my kitchen table, reflecting upon events still to come. I had decided to ring Caroline and take things from there, and wherever *there* should happen to be was OK with me, because I was now cool, calm, collected and sane.

I would ring Caroline and say hello to the mother of my child, because I figured that a hello was as good a place as any to start. I would then follow up my hello with something else, although I'd decided to let Caroline take things from there, because I just had, and besides, I wasn't really sure what should follow on from hello, especially when my reason for ringing Caroline went beyond the norm, dealing as it did with the possibility of a father becoming reacquainted with the daughter he once knew.

Things to do and people to see.

11.50 AM. I sat at my kitchen table drinking a fresh cup of coffee and smoking a cigarette which had come from a newly opened pack of twenty, and I had decided to ring Caroline and say hello. Because lunchtime was fast approaching, I knew that Caroline would probably be working in one of the two restaurants she owns, and I decided to ring the restaurant on Baggot Street first, because it seemed as good a place as any to start.

Things to do and people to see.

12.08 PM. A grown-up, I sat at my kitchen table, having decided to ring the other restaurant first, because I figured that the restaurant on Leeson Street was as good a place as any to start. My fresh cup of coffee was now my fourth cup of coffee, and the cigarette in my hand had come from the pack of twenty that was newly opened. What would I say to Jessica if and when I met her? 'Hello, Chicken, it's me, your Da' might work, although somehow I doubted it, and the reason I doubted it was because it made me sound like a soldier who hadn't been home in sixty years, because of the fact that nobody had thought to tell me and the Japanese/ German/Italian/Leitrim soldier I'd been fighting on a godforsaken island somewhere in the jungles of Asia, or Leitrim, or wherever, that the war had ended sixty years ago, following on from the unconditional surrender of me, Japan, Germany, Italy or Leitrim. On second thoughts, 'Hi' might be a more reasonable way of saying hello to the daughter I hadn't seen in over two years, and if Jessica didn't recognise me, it would probably be because she'd thought it best to forget me, which didn't seem unreasonable, all things considered.

Things to do and people to see.

12.23 PM. I thought it best to ring Caroline after lunch, because lunch was usually a busy time for Caroline, and so I did what I did, which was nothing much, but sometimes nothing much was all I could do. At 12.24 PM the phone rang, and in response to the ringing, I answered the phone, and I was to find myself saying hello to the woman who was the mother of my child. Caroline asked me how I was, and I said that I was fine, and I then asked Caroline how she was, and she said she was fine too. We then spent several minutes discussing this and that, although we spent most of our time talking about our daughter, and Caroline told me that my daughter was going to a birthday party that evening, and I said that was nice, and Caroline said that it was nice, because

Bob O'Meara was a very nice young man. I then asked Caroline about the very nice young man called Bob O'Meara, and Caroline told me that the very nice young man called Bob O'Meara was thirteen, and I didn't say much else about the very nice young man called Bob O'Meara, because the very nice young man called Bob O'Meara was a man, and my daughter was my daughter.

Several times in the past, Caroline had asked me if I would like to drop up to the house for dinner, and my reply had always being in the negative, because the time wasn't right and I wasn't ready. And so it didn't really surprise me when Caroline asked me once more if I might like to drop up to the house for dinner, although my reply this time was somewhat different, because I told Caroline that yes, I'd love to drop up to the house for dinner. Caroline seemed to be somewhat taken aback by a reply that was different from all replies that had preceded it, and she asked me how did Saturday sound, and I told her that Saturday sounded very fine indeed, and I thought it best to avoid making any reference to a grown-up who was terrified at the prospect of meeting his twelve-year-old daughter, because it would probably have sounded slightly odd, and oddness had no place in the brave new world of me.

I then asked Caroline if I should bring something up to the house with me, and Caroline said that the bringing of myself would more than suffice, and I asked her if she was sure, and she said yes. Caroline then reintroduced Jessica into the conversation by telling me about how thrilled my daughter would be when she heard that her father was coming to dinner, and she concluded our conversation by saying 'Shite', and the reason she said 'Shite' was because someone had just dropped a plate of something or other in the background, and when she said that she had to go, I said I understood, and Caroline then told me that she'd see me on Saturday, and I said that I was looking forward to it immensely.

Things to do and people to see.

I sit at my kitchen table. It is Wednesday. In three days' time I will be seeing my daughter again. I am terrified.

38

The clock in front of me goes *tick-tock*. It is Wednesday afternoon.

Following on from a telephone conversation with the mother of my child, I had tried to remain at home, but it didn't seem to suit. Cigarette in one hand, cup of coffee in the other, I had sat at my kitchen table, and that's really all that can be said about myself, a kitchen table and the multitude of thoughts engulfing me.

I found myself thinking about the weather but there was little point, as it was sunny outside, and because the weather was more or less speaking for itself, my thoughts turned away from the weather and headed in the general direction of a Saturday evening that was just around the corner.

I found myself thinking about the meaning of life, but there was little point because I wasn't a rocket scientist or John Travolta, and because life more or less spoke for itself anyway, my thoughts turned away from the meaning of life and gravitated towards the young woman who gave my life meaning.

I was to find myself thinking about a great many things, but there was little point, and that was why the grown-up who would soon be meeting his twelve-year-old daughter went for a walk.

The clock in front of me goes *tick-tock*.

I had left my apartment and walked down the quays,

wearing a pair of shoes that consisted of two shoes, and all was well with the world. Once, several months previously, things hadn't been quite the same, but things are different now, because I am sane.

I walked down a boardwalk, stopping off at a café, and I bought myself a sandwich and a cup of tea. I sat down in front of the café and ate my sandwich and drank my tea, and beneath my feet the River Liffey flowed past as it made its way towards whatever comes next.

A grown-up, I finished my eating and drinking, and, removing mayonnaise from my lips with a paper napkin, I continued on my way.

As I headed towards the near-continuous ticking of a clock, I crossed over O'Connell Bridge, and upon arrival on the other side, I saw that a friend of mine was smiling at people who were mostly black, white and other colours, although my friend wouldn't have noticed any difference, preoccupied as he was with smiling.

I smiled at the friend who was on the other side of the road, unsure if he had seen me, but it didn't really matter, because my friend with the umbrella deserved a smile, and we all had our crosses to bear, even if his was insanity.

And so I now find myself sitting in front of a clock that goes *tick-tock*.

Jim the barman is doing what he usually does, 'Danny Boy' ever-present.

Joe the communist is doing what he usually does, accompanied by a pint of porter.

Everything would be as it should be, if it wasn't for the absence of Frank the barber.

It seems – or so the story goes, as relayed to me by Jim the barman and Joe the communist – that Frank the barber tried to leave this world behind him. Why this should be, they could not say, although I suspected that it had something to do with yesterday, or the day before, or most days subsequent to his birth. Several days ago Frank the barber was walking home when he decided to take a detour from life by visiting the River Liffey.

As his lungs succumbed to the watery shit that flows through my capital city, Frank the barber would probably have been content to leave things as they were, but a stranger who was passing had other ideas, and jumped into the shit and saved him.

Frank the barber is now recuperating in a hospital that is psychiatric, and he has been visited by Jim the barman, Joe the communist and Jesus Christ.

Because Frank the barber is my friend, I will also visit him in the hospital that is psychiatric, although I will ask a nurse for a visitor's pass, in case there is some kind of mix-up.

I do not know who saved my friend Frank. He was probably just someone who saw someone else in the shit and jumped into the shit to save him.

The clock in front of me goes *tick-tock*. I sit side by side with Joe the communist. In front of us are two drinks, one that is soft, and one pint of porter. I know that I will never drink alcohol again because I am now sane, and because of this, I will soon be seeing my daughter again.

But as I look at the pint of porter, I begin to doubt my sanity, and so I decide to leave, because I know that I am not insane, or so the story goes.

Leaving the clock that goes *tick-tock*, I walk along the banks of the Liffey.

Once upon a time, someone other than myself walked where I am walking and decided it was time for closure. Once upon the same once upon a time, a faceless stranger walked along the same path and saved the stranger who was struggling beneath him.

It is Wednesday afternoon, and in three days' time I will be seeing my daughter.

I look across the street and see a man of my acquaintance, and he smiles at me, and I smile at him.

It is Wednesday afternoon and everything is as it should be, save for the detour which was taken by a friend of mine called Frank.

39

A writer, I hold a man's hand. The man is unconscious, knocked out by a concoction of drugs, all of which are designed to keep him that way. I suppose it's difficult to kill yourself when you're knocked out, and so the concoction of drugs probably makes sense.

Frank the barber is wearing a pair of pyjamas that are not his, belonging as they do to the Irish state, and they would have started out life as a darker shade of blue. The darker shade of blue has, over the years, become a lighter shade of blue, and that's just the way of things in the twenty-first century.

Frank the barber shares a ward with people who suffer from mental illnesses of some sort or other. If this was Hollywood, one of them would probably think that they were Napoleon, or someone equally as funny, but the mental hospital that is little more than a couple of miles away from a General Post Office of long ago is grounded firmly in reality, and the overpowering stench of urine isn't something that Napoleon would have identified with.

I hold the hand of my friend Frank, and I am surrounded by fellow citizens who are ill, and such is life.

In time – tomorrow, or the day after – Frank will awaken, and I will talk to my friend Frank, and I can only hope that my friend Frank will talk to me, and if it's not me, I can only hope that he will talk to someone, because

I think that it might be good to talk.

But for the moment he is asleep, and I can do little more than hold the hand of my friend Frank.

40

Psychiatric hospital visited, I arrived home just as Kate Kowolski was arriving home.

Driving the Ford Fiesta of many L-plates into the car park beside our apartment block, she looked for a parking space, which wasn't that difficult because there were only a couple of cars occupying two of the many spaces which were available to her. For reasons best known to herself and rocket scientists, Kate Kowolski decided to park in between the two cars, which were very close together, but I figured that Kate Kowolski knew what she was doing, because the only thing I'd ever learned to drive was a bicycle.

Ignoring the fact that she'd never passed a driving test in her life, Kate Kowolski proceeded to reverse her car into the parking space that was not large, and I did the only thing I could do, which was nothing much, but sometimes nothing much was all I could do, and the only thing I could do in the circumstances as they presented themselves to me involved me standing in front of a car that was now moving backwards. Because I was a writer who knew about things, I then decided to move my right hand in a circular motion, as I indicated to the driver of the car that was now moving backwards that she should lock hard, or do whatever she felt like doing herself, which she probably would anyway, and I couldn't say that I blamed her, because I wasn't entirely sure what I was doing myself.

The two cars on either side of the Ford Fiesta remained unscathed throughout the entire operation, and having successfully negotiated safe passage for herself and her Ford Fiesta through a gap that didn't seem to be there, Kate Kowolski brought her Ford Fiesta to a halt, and I stopped moving my right hand about.

Kate Kowolski than stepped out of her car and said hello, and I said something similar, and she then asked me why I had been waving my hand about, and I asked her what did she mean, and she told me that I'd looked like someone who was conducting a symphony orchestra, and I didn't reply, because she was probably right.

As we walked away from the three cars that were auditioning for a part in a tin of sardines, Kate Kowolski asked me if I'd eaten, and I said yes, before changing my mind and saying no, because I realised that the cup of tea and sandwich I'd consumed earlier that day, on a boardwalk that belonged elsewhere, didn't really count. Because I'd changed my mind and said no, Kate Kowolski told me that she would be sitting down to eat in an hour or so, and she went on to tell me that I was welcome to join her if I was doing nothing else, and I said yes, because I was doing nothing else, and besides, I was hungry, and she looked gorgeous, although that has nothing to do with anything.

One hour later I went to the apartment of my neighbour Kate Kowolski, and I shared a meal with her which consisted of chicken curry and a spicy rice that probably came from somewhere south of Cork, and dessert consisted of hot apple tart and ice cream, and Kate Kowolski also made the coffee because I couldn't make a decent cup of coffee to save my life.

Somewhere between the eating of the curry and the drinking of the coffee, Kate Kowolski asked me what kind of day I'd had, and I told her about how I'd be seeing Jessica in a few days' time, and Kate Kowolski's face lit up with joy upon hearing news of the forthcoming reunion. I also told her about how I was feeling slightly nervous about meeting Jessica again, and Kate Kowolski told me that my nervousness was perfectly understandable, but she told me not to complicate things by thinking too far ahead, although she did say that I should give Jessica a hug when I met her.

Kate Kowolski had asked me about my day, and I'd told her. Other things had happened that day, including the writing of shite and a visit to a psychiatric hospital, but I made no reference to happenings elsewhere, preferring instead to talk about the twelve-year-old daughter who was a ten-year-old daughter when we'd last met.

Somewhere between the eating of the curry and the drinking of the coffee, Kate Kowolski had asked me about what kind of day I'd had, and following the conversation which had resulted from her enquiry, I asked Kate Kowolski about what kind of day she'd had, and Kate Kowolski cried. I asked Kate Kowolski why she was crying, and she suggested that we go for a walk, so I ended up going for a walk in the company of my neighbour Kate Kowolski.

41

It was a nice evening, so we decided to walk to the Phoenix Park. Fifteen minutes after leaving our apartment block, we said goodbye to the city and said hello to trees and bushes and birds and things. Because I was a writer who knew about life, I thought it best not to ask Kate Kowolski why she had been crying until we reached the park, calculating as I did that the trees and bushes and birds and things would allow my neighbour to tell me what was troubling her in surroundings that were mostly silent, save for the occasional car that would pass us by, or the *tweet-tweeting* of birds who would be more than likely doing whatever it is that birds do whenever they go *tweet-tweet*.

Within the Phoenix Park there is a war memorial to people who were mostly young, and it was there that we sat, dwarfed by a stone forget-me-not that was grey, and larger than normal. As is the way with these things, a distant bird went *poo-tee-weet*.

I asked Kate Kowolski what was wrong, and Kate Kowolski proceeded to tell me what was wrong, and what was wrong was Gerald the gobshite. In truth, she never described Gerald as a gobshite in so many words – or in any amount of words, come to think of it – and I knew that Gerald wasn't a gobshite, because his eyes once told me that he was familiar with wallflowers, which was quite unusual, all things considered.

No, Gerald was no gobshite. He was simply the man that Kate Kowolski had lunched with earlier that day, and at that lunch, Kate Kowolski informed Gerald that she didn't think things were working out between them, and that it might be best if they went their separate ways. Because I was a writer who knew about life, I then asked Kate why things hadn't worked out between them, and Kate told me that sometimes things just don't work out, because that's just the way things are. Because I was a writer who was also a male, I then asked Kate to explain to me what she meant, and she said that she couldn't explain to me what she meant, because, she said, sometimes that's just the way things were.

To the west of us, the sun was saying goodbye for a while, and I looked at the woman who was seated beside me. She'd broken up with Gerald, and even though she hadn't had the best of days, this was the woman whose face had unselfishly lit up with joy when I'd told her that I would soon be meeting Jessica again. As is the way with these things, I continued to look at the woman who was seated beside me, because I just did, and I could see the setting sun reflected in eyes that were moist, and I wanted to hold her or something, but I didn't. She shivered, probably because I was continuously looking at her, although there was an outside possibility that her shivering was a result of the evening air that was getting cool. Because she was only wearing an Aran jumper over a dress that was green and yellow and white and blue, I decided to take off my jacket and put it around her shoulders. She thanked me, and the smile on her face told me that her shivering had nothing to do with me, which was probably for the best, I suppose, because at some point in the future I will marry Kate Kowolski, although neither of us could have known it at the time.

I sat with my neighbour Kate Kowolski, and because I

was no longer wearing a jacket, I knew that I'd probably end up with a runny nose tomorrow, but it didn't matter, because I was a man, and such is life.

The sun disappeared somewhere beyond Leitrim, and as we left the memorial to the thousands upon thousands of once-upon-a-time stories that were now mostly forgotten, a gentle breeze came out of nowhere, and the trees around us swayed this way and that. But I chose not to heed the warnings of the gentle breeze, mostly because I was sane, and now utterly dependable.

And so I walked with my neighbour Kate Kowolski out of the Phoenix Park, and I found myself shivering from time to time, because that was just the way of things, I guess.

42

A gentle breeze came from somewhere or other, and such is life.

Thursday. I am writing again, even if the writing is shite. In two days' time I will be seeing my daughter, and all of my dreams will come true. I haven't had a drink for several months, and I've weathered many storms. As someone once said, I did it my way, and things were now as they always should have been. Regrets, I had many, but then again, too many to mention.

Life is good.

Thursday. Two days' time. Jessica.

Yes, life is very good, or so the story goes.

Thursday morning, I went for a walk. It was a nice day for a walk: sunny, with just the faintest hint of a breeze.

Irresponsible. Insane. Two words: nothing complicated.

A long story; a short story.

Once upon a time, followed by whatever comes next.

The clock comes next.

It goes *tick-tock*.

Joe the communist is sitting beside me, and such is life.

On the counter in front of us there are two drinks, and I am grateful that sanity has enabled me to tell the difference between one soft drink and one pint of porter.

Jesus sits in a corner, reflecting on secrets he'll probably take with him to the grave.

I look at the drinks on the counter, reflecting on the relative merits of one soft drink and one pint of porter.

I look in the mirror, and I see reflected back at me a man who once fathered a child.

Jim the barman is doing what he usually does, ensuring the continuing existence of a boy called Danny.

The clock goes *tick-tock*.

The singular pint of porter that sits on the counter is now a half-pint of porter, because that's just the way of things, I guess.

The soft drink is now gone, because Joe the communist likes to start his day by quenching a thirst with something other than porter, and so his drinking a soft drink probably makes sense.

A now-absent soft drink and a half-pint of porter.

And such is life, courtesy of a gentle breeze that came from nowhere.

43

Moo. A cow. I can hear a cow. The cow is far away, but I can still hear it. I'm probably lying in a laneway somewhere, so the cow is somewhat confusing, but mine is not to reason why. What day is it? Not sure. I could be dreaming. It might explain the cow. Moo. A dream involving a cow. What will I think of next? Eyes closed, which is probably for the best. I could be dead. But if I *am* dead, where does the cow come in? The cow must be dead too. I'm in an afterlife for cows. Makes sense. Perhaps the cow was once a person, and having passed on to whatever comes next, the person found themselves reincarnated as a cow. For all I know, I might not be me. I might have been reincarnated also, only to find that I'd been transformed into a duck. Moo. Quack-quack. Grand day, thank God.

Death. Little more than wishful thinking. I am not dead, and such is life. I am alive, or so the story goes, lying in a laneway somewhere, listening to a distant cow go 'Moo.' The ground on which I lie is soft, which is quite unusual, all things considered. Eyes still closed. Better to keep them that way, I think. Not sure what I'd see if I opened my eyes.

I'd probably just see something that I didn't want to see, and so my eyes will remain closed, if only for a time. Moo. Yeah, I think I'll keep my eyes closed, because I'm finding that cow quite confusing. How am I? Difficult to say. I don't usually know how I am until I stand up. I hope it's not

Saturday. I'm meeting Jessica on Saturday. Looking forward to it immensely. I can tell her about the cow. She'd like that.

Throat feels fine, perhaps because I haven't got one, which is probably for the best. My throat has been replaced by the Sahara Desert, and my taste buds tell me that the Sahara Desert is now a toxic-waste dump. Moo. Beats the hell out of me.

'Paul?' Someone is calling out to me. That someone is probably a cow, although I doubt if that would make any sense.

'Paul?' Someone is still calling out to me. Someone is touching me on the arm. I think I'm being touched by a human hand, because it doesn't feel like a hoof.

'Paul, open your eyes.' The someone who is probably not a cow wants me to open my eyes. I have decided to ignore them because they'll probably go away, and even if they don't go away, I'll still ignore them, because it's a free country, and I haven't entirely ruled out the possibility that they could be a cow.

'Paul Conroy, I want you to open your eyes.' The someone who is probably not a cow sounds like a male, which rules out the cow. I have decided to ignore him, her, or whatever, because I just have, and if it should turn out that I have been dreaming, none of this will matter much anyway.

'Paul, I know that you can hear me. Please open your eyes.' Whether man or beast, they are proving to be quite insistent. I hope to hell it's not Saturday, because I'm supposed to be meeting Jessica on Saturday, and I hope to hell that I'm dreaming, because the alternative would mean that I'm mad.

I lie in a laneway somewhere, and in the distance a cow goes 'Moo.' For reasons best known to myself, I have decided to open my right eye, and do whatever comes next.

I try to open my right eye, but my eyelashes are glued together by something or other, and so I set to work on the opening of my left eye, only to find more of the same.

I lie, eyes shut, and in the distance a cow goes 'Moo.' Something comes into contact with my face, and that something feels wet. My face is sore, because the something that is wet is telling me that my face is sore, but I ignore the pain, save for a loud screech that makes a passing reference to same.

The something that is wet has moved onto my eyes and is now gently brushing itself against my eyelashes.

'That's better,' the male who is probably not a cow informs me, and in all likelihood he's telling the truth, because I am in no position to argue.

'Paul?' Yes? I haven't actually said yes, because I'm not sure if I can open my mouth, because my mouth feels like shit, and so I do the only thing I *can* do, which is nothing much, but sometimes nothing much is all I can do, and the only thing I can do in the circumstances is once again to try and open my right eye, which I mostly succeed in doing, thanks to eyelashes which are now moist.

Right eye now opened, I look at the skies above, only to find that the skies above have been replaced by a ceiling that looks very far away. And so it is that I find myself lying in a laneway, looking up at a ceiling that shouldn't really be there, and as is the way with these things, an angel has appeared in front of me. Because I am a writer who knows about life, I know that the angel is an angel because he is dressed entirely in white. In his right hand the angel is holding a sponge, which seems a bit unusual, but that's probably just the way of things in the land of angels.

I can now see that the angel has put down the sponge and is holding a glass of water.

The angel is smiling at me and, lifting my head slightly forward, he is bringing the glass of water into contact with my lips.

My angel is a nice angel, and because he is an angel I know that I am not dreaming: I am alive.

And somewhere in the distance, a cow goes 'Moo.'

44

My angel is called Harold. I think that Harold is probably a psychiatric angel, because Harold comes and goes, comes and goes, always locking the door after him.

I'm not sure what lies beyond that locked door, although I suspect that it might have something to do with insanity.

Thanks to Harold giving me the occasional pill, the animals who usually make their presence felt have, by and large, decided to go on their holidays. I sleep most of the time, and I suspect that has something to do with the pills that are small and white. I don't sleep all the time; in fact, I think I've been known to stay awake for at least ten minutes before falling asleep again. I keep asking Harold what day it is, and Harold asks me why I want to know what day it is, and I start to tell Harold about Jessica, but I don't get very far because I usually fall asleep.

I am in a room which is old, and larger than normal, and I share the room with someone else. I'm not sure who that someone else is, but he seems to sleep most of the time, and he looks like shit. I think that he might be an alcoholic, because he sweats a lot and he has a red nose, although Ray Milland never had a red nose, so I guess that's got nothing to do with anything. Sometimes, when we're both awake, myself and my roommate talk to each other, but our conversations never progress very far, because one of us usually falls asleep. But during a conversation that lasted for about thirty seconds, my roommate told me that I looked like shit, but that's probably because he's mad.

There is a big window in the room, and beyond the bars that are on the window I can see the tops of trees, so I figure that I'm probably in Leitrim or somewhere.

If I need to go to the bathroom, Harold will hold on to me gently, and the two of us will walk arm in arm into the en suite bathroom that is behind another locked door.

Sometimes, because I'm asleep, I won't need to go to the bathroom, and Harold will then do what angels are probably paid to do, and they must get paid quite a lot.

I sleep, and then I wake, and then I fall asleep again. I'm not sure what day it is, because Harold won't tell me, although it's probably getting very close to Saturday.

And somewhere in the distance, a cow goes 'Moo.'

45

Come day, go day.
Wishin' me heart it was Sunday.
Drinkin' buttermilk all the week,
Whiskey on a Sunday.

This morning Harold told me it was Sunday. He didn't say which Sunday exactly.

Just that it was Sunday. No buttermilk. No whiskey. Just more of those little white tablets and a bowl of soup. In recent days, or hours, or periods in time which are best remembered for not being remembered, the tablets have become fewer in number, and consequently I now find myself mostly staying awake. I pass the time by lying in bed, looking out at the treetops that are in Leitrim or somewhere. The man in the bed opposite me is called Dermot, and he's an alcoholic, or so he says. Because it's Sunday, he'll probably be expecting to receive some whiskey, but I doubt if Harold will oblige, which is probably for the best. Dermot is about twenty years older than I am, and yesterday, or the day before, he told me that he was an architect and that he has a wife called Kathleen, a son called Dermot and a daughter called Mary, and having told me almost everything there was to tell me about himself, Dermot asked me if I had any family. I told him that I had had a family once, but that was a long time ago. I talk a lot with Dermot, and Dermot talks a lot with me. Yesterday, or the day before, Dermot asked me if I was an alcoholic, but I didn't say much by way of a reply, because Dermot wouldn't understand about wallflowers and things.

The animal is probably called Daisy. Yesterday, or the day before, I walked over to the window and looked down at Daisy. As I first thought, Daisy is a cow, and she lives in a field not very far away. Daisy was chewing something or other when I looked down at her, and I suspect that it was grass. Daisy has big lips and reminds me of someone or other, but I think it best if I simply refer to Daisy as Daisy, because even though Julia Roberts is also beautiful, I don't think she'd understand.

It is Sunday. Yesterday was Saturday, and I was supposed to meet Jessica on a Saturday.

I'm not sure if the Saturday in question was yesterday's Saturday, because I'm not really sure which Sunday this is.

For reasons best known to himself, Harold now lets me go to the bathroom alone.

There's a mirror in that bathroom, coloured mostly black and blue.

There is little more that can really be said about the situation that currently prevails. I am alive, and I spend most of time talking with Dermot, and Dermot spends most of his time talking with me.

Sometimes, when Dermot's asleep and I'm awake, I'll lie on my bed looking out at the treetops that are probably in Leitrim or somewhere, and beyond a window that is barred, I can occasionally hear Daisy going 'Moo.'

46

Wednesday. I am alone. Yesterday Harold handed Dermot some clothes and sent him on his way. I asked Dermot where he was going, and Dermot told me that he was going downstairs. I then asked Dermot what was downstairs, and Dermot told me that people like us were downstairs. I considered asking Dermot what he meant by this, but I didn't, because Dermot wouldn't understand about wallflowers and things.

I haven't been given any little white tablets for a day or two. I miss the tablets and the sleep, but mine is not to reason why.

Today Harold gave me the first meal I'd had in several days, or months, or whatever, but even though I like chicken, I didn't eat much, because I wasn't really hungry.

This morning I had a shave, probably because I had a beard. I shaved myself with a razor, and Harold stood beside me while I shaved, which was something of a surprise, because I didn't really think I was the sort of person who'd steal a razor.

Wednesday. I am alone, save for the occasional visit from Harold and the vocal outpourings of a neighbour called Daisy.

47

Friday. I recognised the jeans, the shirt, the socks, the underwear and the pair of runners. They were mine, and the last time I'd seen them was in a wardrobe which was in the apartment I used to call home. But they were no longer at home, because they were now sitting on top of the bed I had come to regard as home, and the reason they were sitting there was because Harold had put them there.

I stood beside Harold, looking at the things which belonged elsewhere, and I asked Harold what they were doing on top of the bed. Harold told me that it was now time for me to get dressed, so I asked Harold if I was going home, and Harold told me that I was going downstairs.

Mine is not to reason why, so I got dressed. I thought it best to ask Harold the question which was troubling me, and in response to my query Harold told me that a woman called Caroline had paid a visit to Leitrim earlier that morning, and that was how it had come to pass that the things which belonged in Dublin had made their way to Leitrim, only she hadn't actually gone to Leitrim as such, because Harold told me that I was in Kildare, which probably explains the lack of rain.

I got dressed, and such is life. Harold walked through the door that was usually locked, and I followed soon after. But before I left, I looked back at the bed I had come to regard as home, and I remembered the numerous conversations I'd had with an alcoholic called Dermot.

And so it was that I left the room, and in the distance Daisy did what she mostly did, which was talk quite a lot.

48

The house was a big house, and many people lived there. Harold clearly knew his way around the place, because he showed little indication that he would get lost, and so I followed in his footsteps, en route to whatever came next.

Whatever came next was a dormitory, but before we arrived there we had to make our way down two flight of stairs and walk through several corridors. Each corridor contained many doors, some closed, some half-open. Behind some of the doors that were half-open, I could see that people were sitting around in small groupings, no doubt discussing the weather, and because this wasn't Leitrim, there wouldn't really have been that much to discuss. But even though I was in a place other than Leitrim, it was quite apparent to me that the weather was proving to be a pretty emotive issue, because some of the people were crying and some of the people were shouting, but that's probably just the way of things when you're not in Leitrim.

The house was an old house, and once upon a time in the past it looked like it belonged to Lord Such-and-such. Having reached an age in which youth played no part, Lord Such-and-such would then have done the decent thing and passed on to whatever comes next. As is the way of these things, the house would have been inherited by a younger version of the Lord who was now absent, and somewhere between then and now the house would have been sold and transformed into what it had now become: a collection of many doors, some closed, some half-open; chambers which contained people who were emotionally discussing this, that and the weather.

The dormitory had about twelve beds in it, and beside each bed there was a bedside locker, and beside each bedside locker there was a wardrobe. Some of the wardrobes had photographs attached to them and all of the people in the photographs were smiling, probably because it had stopped raining. The children were the ones who seemed to be smiling most, and that's as it should be, I think.

Above each bed there was a framed request to whoever is in charge of the known universe and Leitrim: a simple prayer which requested nothing more than peace of mind and the ability to roll with the punches where possible, because more often than not there's little that can be done to change them.

Harold led me to a bed at the end of the dormitory, informing me that it was mine.

As he opened the wardrobe beside my bed, I could see that it contained clothing that all belonged to me, and because I wasn't a rocket scientist, I came to the conclusion that the clothing had managed to make its way from Dublin to someplace other than Leitrim, in much the same way that the clothing I was now wearing had managed to make its way from Dublin to someplace other than Leitrim.

Harold then told me that he'd leave me, as it was time for him to go. I asked him if I'd see him again, and he said that I probably would, although he told me that he mostly worked upstairs. I didn't really know Harold all that well, so it came as something of a surprise to me when I found that I had become the recipient of a hug from Harold: an embrace which was accompanied by a statement to the effect that today was the first day of the rest of my life. Because I was a writer who knew about life, I was only too well aware of the fact that Harold had done little more than state the obvious, because if yesterday had been the first day of the rest of my life, today would have been the second day of the rest of my life, and that wouldn't have made much sense. But not wishing to offend, I simply nodded at Harold in agreement, and the reason I didn't want to cause offence was because I liked Harold, and once upon a time in the past he had been the angel who'd brought a cup of water into contact with lips that were parched.

Harold then left, and that was that.

Sitting down on the side of my bed, I surveyed my surroundings. With one exception, all of the other beds were neatly made, and the windows in the dormitory had no bars on them, probably because of an oversight. The photographic images of many smiling faces all seemed to be looking in my direction, but that's probably because I was the only other person present. I knew that no one else was present, because I had a good instinct for these things, until I discovered that I wasn't the only other person present, which shouldn't really have come as a surprise.

Several beds removed, there was the single unmade bed, and the reason the bed was unmade was that there was someone under the covers. Using every power of deduction that was available to me, I knew instinctively that the person under the covers was not a happy camper, although his introductory remark did help somewhat.

'Bastards' was the remark that gave the game away, and I didn't say or do anything, because I wasn't sure what I could have said or done. Instead, I did the only thing I could do, which was nothing much, which was much the same, and so I sat on the bed, looking at distant bedcovers that occasionally tossed and turned.

'Fucking . . . bastards' now followed on from the remark that had preceded it, and I found myself looking around the room for assistance, but there was no assistance forthcoming, because photographs aren't really much use, even if they contain smiling faces.

Much to my surprise, I decided that it was time to take some action, so I asked the distant person who was under the covers if they were OK, which they clearly weren't, but I had to start somewhere.

'Fuck them' was the reply to my query into the current status of the life of whoever, so I decided to give the matter a great deal of thought before embarking upon whatever course of action I thought should come next. But I didn't have to do anything else, because no other words were spoken, replaced as they were by a gentle sobbing.

I was relieved that no action was required on my part, so I found myself wondering just what in hell did I think I was doing as I walked towards the sound of gentle sobbing, and my sense of wonderment was not lessened to any great degree when I found myself sitting down on the side of a bed which belonged to a total stranger.

'Erm . . . ' Florence Nightingale said, as he sat on the side of the bed. I'm sure there were other things I could have said, but I couldn't think of any of them, and so 'Erm . . . ' seemed quite appropriate.

'Go away' was the muffled instruction to Florence Nightingale. Florence Nightingale considered his position, and retreat seemed a reasonable option. But would Florence Nightingale listen to Florence Nightingale? No. Instead, Florence Nightingale was to find himself sitting in a very strange place, engaging in a perfectly rational conversation.

'Go away.' (muffled) 'No.' 'Go . . . away.' (muffled) 'No.' 'Just . . . just fuck off.' (muffled, although slightly louder)

'No.' 'Get lost.' (muffled, but now slightly subdued) 'No.' 'Why don't you pleeease just leave me alone? Pleeease?' 'No.' There now followed a slight lull in the conversation, which was probably for the best, all things considered. I sat and waited, wondering about nothing in particular, knowing that the next move was not up to me. Much to my surprise – and breaking all known precedents – I was proven correct, as a head appeared from beneath the bedcovers. The head belonged to a young man of about twenty, and he looked at me and I looked at him.

For reasons best known to myself and Donald Duck, I could sense that this was a young man who simply needed a shoulder to cry on, and because my shoulders were the nearest ones to hand, I decided to make them available to him.

'Just who the fuck are you?' True, it wasn't the best of starts, but at least it was something.

'Hi, I'm Paul,' I said, putting forward my right hand in anticipation of a handshake.

'Well, Paul, will you do me one small favour?' Even though my attempt at a handshake had been rebuffed, I didn't take it too personally, and if this kid wanted me to do him one small favour, it seemed like the decent thing to do.

'A favour? Yes, I'd be delighted to.' 'Well, Paul, please go fuck yourself.' Because masturbation had not been part of Plan A, and I hadn't really got a Plan B, I decided to invoke Plan A (Subsection 2), although I didn't really know what I was doing, and so I decided to act as if this was a perfectly normal, run-of-the-mill situation, which for the most part it wasn't. Besides, I hadn't had a cigarette since forever.

'Have you got a smoke?' (Plan A, Subsection 2) 'What?' 'A cigarette? Have you got one?' 'You're not going to go away, are you?' 'Tell you what, I'll go away if you'll give me a smoke.' 'One smoke?' 'Yes.' 'And then you'll go away?' 'Yes.'

'OK, one smoke and you're out of here, yeah?' 'Absolutely.'
The young man reached out and, opening a bedside locker,
produced a half-empty pack of twenty. He removed a cigarette
from the half-empty pack of twenty and handed it to me. I
thanked him, although I was to remain seated, because we
still had some unfinished business to get through.

'What?' he said.

'What?' I said.

'What the fuck are you doing still sitting there?' 'A light.'
'What?' 'I need a light.' 'You said nothing about a light.'
'Must have forgotten to mention it.' 'You haven't got a light?'
'No.' 'Jesus Christ, will somebody *please* save me from this
man.' Reaching into his bedside locker, my new roommate
produced a box of matches and handed them to me. I thanked
him, and did the same as before, which was nothing much,
but that's OK.

'Yesss?' he enquired, and I can't say I blamed him.

'An ashtray.' 'What?' 'I need an ashtray.' 'Are you fucking
with me?' 'Want the truth?' 'Yes, please.' 'Yes, I am absolutely,
100 per cent fucking with you. Although I do need an ashtray.'
'Who *are* you?' 'I'm new.' 'You don't say.' 'I do say.' 'You're not
going to go away, are you?' 'No.' 'Why?' 'No reason. It's just
that you seemed a bit upset, and I was wondering if I could
help.' 'Well, there's feck all you can do. Bastards.' 'Bastards?'
'Yes, bastards.' 'What bastards?' 'They all are.' 'Who are?' *'Those*
bastards,' my roommate informed me, as he pointed in the
general direction of everything surrounding him.

'What did they do?' 'Oh, nothing much. I said I was going
home, and they asked me why, and I said I was too young for
this shit, and they accused me of being in denial, and I said
I wasn't in denial, and they said I was in denial, and I said I
just wanted to go home, and they said I shouldn't, and I said
"Fuck you."' 'In denial about what?' 'Jesus, you *are* new.' 'Yeah,

although I feel quite old.' 'Face up to the fact that I have a drink problem, they told me. Bastards.' 'Have you got a drink problem?' 'No, I'm in here on holiday. Considered Barbados, but I don't like the sun. Of course I've got a drink problem. Wouldn't be in this godforsaken place if I didn't.' 'So you know you've got a drink problem, but others are telling you that you don't know that you've got a drink problem, and that's more or less that?' 'Yes.' 'Sounds complicated.' 'No shit.' 'What are you going to do?' 'I'm outta here. Fuck the lot of them.' 'Where are you going to go? Barbados?' 'Stop fucking with me.' 'I'm not fucking with you.' 'You *are* fucking with me.' 'I'm not.' 'Yes you are.' 'No I'm not.' 'Who the fuck *are* you?' 'Oh, no one in particular. Just someone who's a bit of a screw-up.' 'Yeah, well, alcoholism can do that to you.' 'Well actually, I'm not an alcoholic. I mean, yeah, I drink, but mostly I don't drink.' 'Christ, they're going to *love* you.' 'Who?' 'The same bastards who love *me*.' 'Are they that bad?' 'Bad doesn't even *begin* to describe them.' 'So you're leaving?' 'Yeah, and if you want my advice, you'll get the hell out of here too.' 'Tell you what.' 'What?' 'Let's have a smoke, and then we can go.' 'Why?' 'Well, I haven't had a smoke in ages, and I'd enjoy the company.' 'One smoke?' 'Yeah.' 'You're fucking with me again, aren't you?' 'Absolutely.' 'Figures.' Whether it figured or not, my new roommate smiled at me for the first time since we'd met, and as we smoked his cigarettes, he told me about himself, and I told him about myself. My new friend was called Daragh, and in two months' time he would be twenty-one. Daragh was very young, but that probably had nothing to do with anything, although I wasn't really sure what had.

Suffice to say that the two of us just talked and smoked, and sometimes the best you can do is all you can do.

49

Twenty-eight days. Not long. In retrospect, the first twenty-seven days were mostly indistinguishable from one another, involving as they did discussions about the weather, and visits from people who knew me, once upon a time in the past. On the twenty-eighth day I looked in the mirror, and because of this things worked out just grand.

Day 1
Having smoked Daragh's pack of cigarettes to a state of extinction, we went for a walk outside. Outside was quite large, containing as it did gardens that were manicured, and birds and trees and alcoholics and things. There were many people to be found outside, all of them walking and talking. The people said hello to me and I said hello to them.

Daragh didn't say hello to anyone, probably because he wanted to go home.

As I was now on the outside, I was able to look back at what had once been my inside. The house was old, although I knew that it was not my house, because my house existed elsewhere, waiting patiently for the resumption of Chapter 1. There was also another house, but that was of another time, when I will be older than I am now.

Somewhere beside that other house there will be a river bank, and it will be there that I will sit, alongside a neighbour who will have become my wife. And the two of us will look on, as a child who has yet to be born plays the games that children play, because that's just the way of things, I guess.

But that is of the future, and in the present, myself and Daragh went for a walk amidst birds and trees and alcoholics and things.

Leaving the gardens that were manicured behind us, we found ourselves walking down a country lane that bore little resemblance to any laneways I had previously come across.

The laneway was small, and narrower than usual, and on each side of it there were green hedges, and it was there that I happened upon an old friend who was beautiful. Reaching across one of the green hedges I stroked her forehead, but she didn't seem to mind, probably because she was chewing grass.

As I looked at Daisy and Daisy looked at me, a fly landed on Daisy's nose, but Daisy ignored the fly and simply kept on chewing.

And so it came to pass that, in a place other than Leitrim, I found myself in the company of a cow and a young alcoholic, and everything was now grand, because I had nowhere else to go.

Having said goodbye to Daisy, I left the outside and returned with Daragh to the inside.

It was teatime when we returned to the inside, so I went into a room that looked like a restaurant, and Daragh and I had our tea. The man who once shared a room with me joined us at our table, and myself and Dermot and Daragh talked for a long time, and none of us fell asleep. Daragh said that he was leaving tomorrow and I said that was OK, because tomorrow sounded better than today.

The day ended with my going to bed in a room which was full of alcoholics, and in the distance Daisy did what Daisy usually did, which was talk quite a lot.

And so it came to pass that I was to find myself in County Kildare, embarking on a voyage of whatever. What lay ahead of me was something of a mystery, although the future will tell me that the past wasn't quite as complicated as it first seemed.

50

Day 2 (and everything subsequent)
It's a long story; a short story.

The days came and went, and I was to find myself spending most of them in a room, surrounded by Dermot and Daragh and other alcoholics. Sometimes, behind a door which was usually closed, I would find myself talking. Sometimes I would say a lot, sometimes I would say very little. Sometimes I would be told that I was talking shite, sometimes I wouldn't. Jim never accused me of talking shite. Jim was nice. He had a beard, and he told me that he was a counsellor. He also told me that he was an alcoholic, but I guess that's OK. There were those in the room who said I was in denial, but I simply told them the truth as I saw it – and what I saw was a man who, for the most part, didn't drink, and I knew that alcoholics usually did more than that. And so I talked and I listened, counting the days until I could return home and start life anew.

My face was still bruised, but Jim told me not to worry about the bruises. It's the pain inside that matters most – that's what Jim told me. He was also smiling at the time, which seemed a bit strange, but there you have it.

Because the house was a big house, I took Jim aside one day and asked him who was paying my bill. I knew that the bill would be a big bill, because little bills don't normally enter into the equation in big houses. In response to my query, Jim told me who was paying my bill, and upon hearing his answer, I knew that once I had made my return to the world outside, I would probably have to get a job doing something or other, somewhere or other, because I now owed Caroline quite a lot of money.

I usually had lunch with Daragh and Dermot. The menu was varied, consisting as it did of bacon and cabbage, or cabbage and bacon. There was always fish on Friday, but that's probably because we were in County Kildare. Daragh wanted to go home most days, but Dermot and I managed to turn most days into the following day.

Once a week someone from the outside would come to the inside to talk with us.

These people from the outside always seemed to be smiling, which seemed a bit unusual, but mine is not to reason why. They would tell us about how they had once been on the inside, and they would then follow that up by telling us about how they were managing to survive on the outside. This usually involved smiling a lot, drinking coffee, and making sure that Tuesday was always Tuesday and not Wednesday, which on the face of it seemed a bit obvious, but because they were from the outside and I was from the inside, I didn't feel in a particularly strong position to argue, so I just let things be.

The first person to come in from the outside to talk with us was a man. He smiled a lot, but that wasn't unusual. The second person to come in from the outside to talk with us was a woman. She smiled a lot, but that's probably because she was also taking Prozac. The third person to come in from the outside to talk with us was something of a surprise. He was a man, although that wasn't really a surprise, because for the most part the chances of someone being male are probably fifty-fifty. He also smiled a lot, although that wasn't really a surprise, because to have done otherwise wouldn't have made much sense at all. No, the surprise lay elsewhere, and it occurred soon after I received my first visitor.

Having eaten lunch (cabbage and bacon, followed by mince pies and custard), I was walking around the gardens, and Dermot and I were doing our usual, as we tried to persuade Daragh to stay just one more day. Outside the big house I could see that a car had just been parked. I didn't pay much attention to the car, because cars were always being parked outside the big house, and besides, Daragh was quite insistent that he was getting the fuck out of there. As is the way with these things, the driver got out of the car, but as is most certainly not the way with these things, I recognised the driver of the car, because the driver of the car was Gerald the gobshite, and I found myself wondering what Gerald the gobshite was doing parking his car outside a big house in County Kildare. Perhaps he was on his way to Leitrim or somewhere, and having found himself lost, he'd decided to stop outside a big house so that he could ask for directions.

If that was indeed the case, he'd obviously decided to ask directions from me, because soon after he'd stepped out of his car he walked across the lawn, and soon after that I was to find myself standing face to face with Gerald the gobshite.

He said hello, and I said hello, and I then introduced him to Dermot and Daragh.

Dermot said hello, but Daragh didn't say hello, probably because he wanted to go home.

Gerald the gobshite then suggested that he and I go for a walk, and I said fine, although I told him that it would have to be a quick walk, because I explained to him that this was the day when someone from the outside would come inside to talk with us. Gerald the gobshite said that he understood, so I went for a walk with Gerald the gobshite.

Leaving the world of the big house behind us, we went for a walk down my favourite laneway. Because it was lunchtime, Daisy paid little heed to us as we passed by, preferring instead to chew whatever it was that she was chewing, while simultaneously removing a fly from her backside, thanks to a tail that went swish.

The laneway was a long laneway, and it seemed to go on forever. Prior to my walk with Gerald the gobshite, I'd never ventured beyond the field of Daisy, so it came as something of a surprise to me when we came across a river.

Standing side by side on a river bank with Gerald the gobshite, he asked me how I was, and I told him that I didn't really know how I was, which wasn't a lie, because I didn't.

I then asked him how he was, and he said that he was grand, and I told him that I was sorry to hear about himself and Kate breaking up, and he said these things happen.

In truth, few words were exchanged between us. Instead, we just stood on a river bank, content to watch the water flow by, as it made its way towards whatever comes next.

After a time, and for no reason in particular, I picked up a stone that was at my feet and threw it across the water. It took one bounce and then went skip-skip-skip as it skimmed across the water. Gerald, clearly impressed, picked up a stone of his own and threw it across the water. His stone also took one bounce, but then went plop as it disappeared, never to be seen again. He looked at the ripples which had been caused by the plop, but he didn't seem to be too upset. He just looked at me and smiled. He also said something to me, and what he said was this: 'Paul, I'm an alcoholic.' That's what he said: nothing too complicated. I didn't say anything by way of a reply, because I didn't know what to say. I could have suggested to him that he go into a big house somewhere and get help, but I decided not to, which was probably for the best.

'I think it's time we were heading back,' was the next thing he said, and he smiled at me as he said it, which seemed slightly mad.

'Yeah, we'd better go. We've got someone coming in to talk with us,' I said, not wishing to complicate things too much, although I wasn't telling a lie, because today was indeed the day of smiling faces and Prozac.

And so we left the river bank and returned elsewhere.

I had stood on a river bank with Gerald the gobshite and watched a river go by. On the far side of that river bank there was something else, but I hadn't paid much heed to the old house that was little more than a shell. At some point in the future, I may well return to that river bank in the company of two other people, and I will leave them, if only for a time – an hour or two at most. And I will walk up a laneway which leads elsewhere, and do what I have to do, because people once did it for me. And having talked to the people on the inside, I will return to the river bank, to people I love, because that's just the way things will be.

But the house that sits beside that river is of little importance for now, and in the now, I returned to the big house in the company of Gerald, the man who had come in from the outside to talk with us.

And the tale he told was a simple tale, involving as it did a wallflower, and I recognised that wallflower, because I had one of my own.

51

One day I walked into a room. The room was quite full, containing as it did many alcoholics, as well as other people, which was something of a surprise.

Dermot's wife and children were in the room, as were the parents of a twenty-year-old who would be leaving tomorrow. Caroline looked well, as did my neighbour Kate Kowolski.

Tom O'Brien also looked well, although that's probably got nothing to do with the fact that he was my agent.

Those on the inside were asked by Jim the counsellor to sit on one side of the room, and those who had come in from the outside were asked to sit on the other side of the room.

Jim the counsellor then asked Dermot's wife and children if they had anything to say, and amidst tears that were many, they informed Dermot that he was killing them, and this was largely due to the fact that he was a husband and father who spent most of his time trying to kill himself. Dermot said nothing. He cried, which was probably all he could do, and I guess that sometimes all you can do is the best you can do.

Jim the counsellor then asked Daragh's parents if they had anything to say, but they mostly cried, although a reference was made to their current state of health and to nervous breakdowns which couldn't have been far away, and by the looks of them I'd say they were both now older than they had once been. Daragh walked over to his parents and hugged them, and I do believe that a hug exchanged within the confines of today probably lasts forever, because tomorrow has yet to be written.

And then it was me.

Caroline told the room that she was the mother of my child, and even though our relationship was now over, she talked about how she still loved me, because she always would. She then talked about our daughter, making reference to the fact that she knew that I loved her. Caroline spoke of many things, and finished by saying that it would soon be time for her to let go of me, because it was the only thing she could do.

Caroline spoke, and Caroline cried, and when she cried, the father of her child cried with her.

Kate Kowolski told the room that she was my neighbour, and even though we had only known each other for a couple of years, I was a friend who had always been there for her, and because of this, she said she felt guilty that she couldn't be there for me. But she now knew that she could never have been there for me, because she had learnt I was suffering from a disease which usually ignores outside influences, although this did not lessen her pain to any great degree. She told the room about picking me up and putting me to bed, and how it hurt like hell, because she was my friend. Kate also cried, and I cried too, although my tears were now continuous, indistinguishable from tears that had gone before.

Tom O'Brien, probably because he was my agent, also cried. He told the room about a friendship that had spanned the decades, and how he had also felt guilty about his inability to be there when it mattered most. But he now knew, he said, that there was little that could have been done, because he was my agent, and not a fucking miracle worker.

And that was that. A simple story: nothing too complicated.

I went into the restaurant with those who had spoken to, and about, me, and the four of us had coffee and biscuits. We talked about this, that and the weather, and I said how I was looking forward to going home, so that I could start writing again. Tom asked the two ladies who were seated with us to excuse his language, before informing me to fuck the writing, because none of it mattered.

I then asked them about how it had come to pass that I had ended up in County Kildare, and Kate Kowolski told me that she'd found me unconscious in the car park of our apartment block one morning, and how this had led to a trip in an ambulance, which had led to a hospital, which had led to here.

I apologised to the people who were seated with me for everything I had, or hadn't, done, and they said that was OK, although I suspect that they had their fingers crossed at the time.

Their visit ended with a walk into the outside, and before they left I hugged Caroline and Kate, and Tom hugged me, although that's probably because of the fact that he was my agent.

Other hugs were being exchanged that day, and I could only hope that for all concerned, everything worked out just grand. But sometimes things might not work out so grand, but even if that is indeed the case, there's little I can do, because the future will tell me that I'm not a rocket scientist, because I'm just me, but because I'm just me, I'm doing OK.

52

Day 28

I went to say goodbye to Daisy today. A beautiful woman was with me. We walked hand in hand down a laneway, and I knew that everything would be grand.

Daisy had very little to say for herself, probably because she was chewing grass. I stroked Daisy on the forehead, as did the beautiful woman who was with me.

I said goodbye to Daisy and went on my way, accompanied by the woman who is beautiful.

At some point in the future, this beautiful young woman will have a daughter, and I will watch her child play as I sit on a river bank in the company of another.

But now is now, and in the now the beautiful young woman is my twelve-year-old daughter, and so I can do little more than walk hand in hand with Jessica, because I'm her father and I love her.

53

I cleared out my wardrobe and said goodbye to alcoholics who had come after me.

Dermot had lasted the twenty-eight days, and had returned to his family several days before. Daragh didn't last twenty-eight days. Instead he lasted one day after another, always knowing that he would be going home tomorrow. Eventually, the one day after another added up to twenty-eight days, and I know that Daragh will be OK, because this story is partially written in the future, and when I am old I will still be friends with Daragh, because he'll need me and I'll need him.

Having collected my things, I said goodbye to Jim the counsellor. He wished me luck and told me that he would always be there if I needed him. I told him I'd be grand, which was a lie, because I was terrified. I then walked upstairs and said goodbye to Harold. We met on the landing, and as he wished me luck he asked me about my plans for the future. I told Harold that as soon as I got home I would start writing again. Harold smiled and shook my hand before asking me if he could show me something. Not wishing to offend, I said yes, and opening a door that was locked, Harold walked into a room and I followed soon after.

The room was old, and larger than normal, and it contained two beds. I recognised the room from a long time ago. I also recognised the beds.

Half-asleep, half-awake, a man was tossing and turning on one of the beds, dancing a dance of death. Harold pointed at the man and asked me if I recognised him. I told Harold the truth, saying that I'd never seen the man before in my life. Harold then told me to take a closer look, so I did, walking up to a bed that smelt mostly of urine and sweat.

As I looked at the man, I also found myself looking into a mirror, and I shook. Harold put his arm around me and asked me if I was OK. I didn't tell Harold that I was OK.

Instead, I thanked Harold for showing me something concerning myself, and Harold told me that no thanks were necessary, because he was just doing his job.

I left the upstairs and walked downstairs. So that's the deal, I thought to myself. No big deal, really; nothing too complicated.

Two people were waiting for me on the outside. Caroline could see that there were tears in my eyes, and so she asked me if I was OK. I can't honestly recall if I said anything, but I think I probably smiled and hugged her. The one thing I do remember is lifting Jessica off the ground, probably because it just seemed like the right thing to do, and this led to a father receiving a kiss from his daughter.

And that was that. A simple story; nothing too complicated – because I'm not a bloody rocket scientist.

54

The clock in front of me goes *tick-tock*.

Occasionally, from time to time, I will find myself sitting in front of the clock, because that's just the way of things, I guess. Strictly speaking, I'm probably not supposed to go anywhere near the sound of ticking clocks, but I do, because that's where some of my friends are. But I don't stay too long, because Jim the barman makes a pretty lousy cup of coffee. Sometimes I go elsewhere, and behind doors which are usually closed, I will find myself discussing the weather in Leitrim, or wherever, with Gerald the gobshite, Frank the barber and others.

I am not sane. I am not insane. I'm just me, and that's OK.

I write, and sometimes I don't, but mostly I do.

Depending on when this is written, I may or may not be married to my neighbour Kate Kowolski. It doesn't really matter. What matters most is that there will be a time when I tell her that I love her, and in response to same, Kate Kowolski will say that she loves me too, and she will be wearing a dress that is coloured green and orange and pink and purple when she says it. But when we get married she will be wearing a white wedding dress and I'll be dressed like a bloody penguin (Kate's idea, although Caroline didn't exactly disagree), and Tom O'Brien will be my best man, and he'll look very strange.

Depending on her age, Jessica will come and go, come

and go, always knowing that she has a father who loves her.

Caroline, regardless of age, will always be Caroline, and I will love her, simply because of who she is.

Tom O'Brien will always be fat, probably because he is my agent. He will marry Suzanne Charles, and I'll be Tom's best man. Claire Casey will be one of Suzanne's bridesmaids and I will dance with Claire at the wedding, although it will be a slow dance, because I'm not John Travolta.

But most of all, there will be life, and that's OK, because to have anything else wouldn't make much sense at all.

*

This part of the story probably hasn't happened yet, but I can't be entirely certain, and because it's set in the future, one can only speculate. But if it did happen, it probably went something like this.

I am an old man sitting by a fireside. A lifetime slips by to the sound of happiness and sadness, laughter and tears.

I close my eyes to the sound of *tick-tock*, and I remember the books: some good, some perhaps not so good. Either way, it doesn't matter. They were mine.

The *tick-tock*, *tick-tock* of my life has slowed in recent years and, eyes closed, I know that what once was is no longer present.

Tick, followed by nothing.

Perhaps the *tick* is to be followed by a *tock*; perhaps not.

Eyes closed, it is now time for me to take my leave.

Memories: some good, some bad. Either way, it doesn't matter. They were mine.

Tick (enter Jim the barman stage right) . . . *tock*.

Jim the barman, Joe the communist, Frank the barber and a man with an umbrella.

It is time.

Memories of many things, but most of all, memories of love.

I once wrote a book. It was a simple book: nothing too complicated.

It opened with four words, and those four words were pretty predictable: 'There is a house.'